TEMPORARY BOOK COLLECTION

On week of: 11/01/09
Send to: MOSQ

On week of: 05/01/10
Send to: SHLK

On week of: 01/01/10
Send to: PINE

On week of: 07/01/10
Send to: BCR1

On week of: 03/01/10
Send to: AUB

On week of:
Send to:

Run B69
Return to FHQ on week of: 09/01/10

THREE
KILLERS

**Center Point
Large Print**

**This Large Print Book carries the
Seal of Approval of N.A.V.H.**

THREE KILLERS

ELI COLTER

CENTER POINT PUBLISHING
THORNDIKE, MAINE

This Center Point Large Print edition
is published in the year 2009 by arrangement with
Golden West Literary Agency.

The text of this Large Print edition is unabridged.
In other aspects, this book may vary
from the original edition.
Printed in the United States of America.
Set in 16-point Times New Roman type.

ISBN: 978-1-60285-519-9

Library of Congress Cataloging-in-Publication Data

Colter, Eli.
  Three killers / Eli Colter.
    p. cm.
  ISBN 978-1-60285-519-9 (library binding : alk. paper)
  1. Large type books. I. Title.

PS3505.O368T47 2009
813'.52--dc22

2009010669

CONTENTS

THREE KILLERS

CHAPTER I
THE MAN OF TERROR

CANYON CENTER was saturated with fear, literally steeped in it. Seldom does the whole population of a town suffer the same enervating dread of the same thing, as was the case in Canyon Center. Crook Alvord said that every man in the place was scared blue, and his exaggeration was slight. Mention the name of Butcher Krantz and any man in the town would turn pale and reach for his gun, or for both of them if he carried two.

Granted, there had at one time been many more men in Canyon Center than there were now. The town was situated in the immutable hills of the West. Round about it rose the mighty forests of Oregon, blanketing gulches and canyons, mountains and hills. Pine, fir, spruce and tamarack spread their pungent perfume in the clean air, and here and there along the creeks tall balsam poplars, studded with sticky buds in the spring, gave off a scent as sweet as vaporized honey. In such a setting, any mining town must be rich in atmosphere. Canyon Center was.

Yet, to an impartial eye, it barely avoided the stigma of being labeled ghost town, because of the little life left in its old bones. The town had only one main street. Only one of its many saloons still survived, the Happy Daze, where Crook Alvord tended bar. Strung along on either side of a single dusty narrow road, numerous deserted slab cabins with warped shake roofs peered stolidly at nothing in particular. Across from the Happy Daze the old Blazin' Sin stood empty and forsaken, its windows boarded up, its doors nailed shut. Farther down the street the once garish Lady Luck no more housed gamblers and ladies of the honky-tonk, but had sunk shamefacedly to the humble and prosaic position of Biddy Gallagher's restaurant. Taking it by and large, Canyon Center was a pretty forlorn little burgh.

Doubtless the fear that rode it seemed all the more ghastly because of those empty peering windows, behind which shadows lurked, dust lay thick, and the sinister spectres of bygone days walked stealthily.

Like all similar boom towns grown gray and no longer booming, Canyon Center had its legends. One of them was the legend of the Lost Cabin Mine. Somewhere back of those gulches and ravines a miner had built a cabin in the center of a canyon bed, long years ago. Panning around feverishly, with the luck that comes once in a lifetime, he had discovered that a ridge at the edge of the canyon bore a vein of free milling ore fabulously rich with gold. The miner had come into the newly risen boom town for provisions, and when he wanted to return to his claim he could find neither cabin nor canyon again.

He came back to town with that story on his tongue and the mad light of frustration beating in his eyes. It must have sounded wholly absurd to those old hillbillies who could track a deer by a fallen twig. Insane, to say a man couldn't return to his own diggings, couldn't find his own claim. Insane to say that a man could not return to the gully he himself had located, in which he had discovered a mine of incalculable wealth. Insane or not, he never found it again, and no other man ever found it either.

Of course, the man was young, and his were doubtless the failings of youth. He had, to all accounts, been terribly excited, and though he declared he came in solely for provisions on that momentous trip, every man who talked to him knew that the actual purpose of the day in town was to have assayed the sample he had brought in from the mines. His excitement was apparent in everything he said and did, mostly because he tried to appear so casual and couldn't. Somebody learned from the assayer later that the ore the youngster had brought in assayed an almost unbelievable value to the ton. A fevered interest ran through the town, and the young man would have had plenty of company in his gulch if anyone had known how to get there. But no one did. They could only wait for him to return to town. Which he did much sooner than they had expected.

But it was only to tell the dismaying story that he couldn't find his gulch again. All gulches and hills looked so much alike. Of course they would, in some parts of that country, some of the older men agreed, especially to a rather green youngster like him. The trouble was, they guessed shrewdly, he had been so excited over his mine that he hadn't thought to take his bearings by the landmarks as he came out. He went back to try to find it again, and several of the experienced hillmen went with him. Absolutely all trace of the mine eluded them. They only knew it was somewhere in the general direction of the Saw Tooth Mountains. They were forced to give up the search finally; and the young prospector, disheartened and discouraged, went wandering out into the hills. No one ever knew what became of him.

He went crazy, likely, was the general opinion, and died out in the hills. Lots of fellows went by the board that way. Seldom a year went by that one or two men didn't go into the hills never to return. Every once in a while, in later years, men would come upon a skeleton where some unfortunate miner had died from injury, had lost his way and starved, or had died of exposure. It became habitual for Canyon Centerites to mark past years by mention of some man who had gone into the hills to die or disappear there. You'd hear one say, "That was the year Ben Halliday went out and never came back." Or another, "That was the y'ar Jesse Laufflin broke his leg an' died in White Horse Gulch, an' wan't found till weeks afterward."

The year that the young man lost his mine and never could find it again came to be known as the year in which old Pegleg Miller went into the hills and never came back. Pegleg was a poor old half cracked prospector who was always going to strike it rich and never did. He had had his leg blown off in a blast he set to crack up a rock ledge. It had nearly killed him, it was all his partner could do to send for help and get a doctor there in time. Doctors weren't too plentiful on the frontier in those days. The doctor they brought Pegleg wouldn't have known a diploma had he seen one. He knew far more about doctoring horses than he did about doctoring people, and was rather rough in his methods. But he saved Miller's life. Some of the men said that that would put a stop to Miller's prospecting. They had called him Black Powder Miller till then.

But Black Powder fooled them. He strapped on a pegleg and went right on prospecting, still swearing he was going to make his strike. The pegleg he himself made, of a tree limb and a piece of harness breeching, a stout and serviceable substitute for a leg, and from then on he was known as Pegleg Miller. He became a familiar sight in the then booming town, stumping about from store to

13

store to gather up provisions, then off on another trek looking for that bonanza he could never relinquish hope of finding. Until the year he went into the hills never to return.

The story of the Lost Cabin Mine became one of the stock legends of Canyon Center, at which passing strangers in later years raised a skeptical eyebrow. But no man ever turned up his nose at the legend of Butcher Krantz, because it was far more than a mere oft-told tale. On two or three different occasions he had been heard to say that there was only one place to which he *knew* he was going someday, and that was Canyon Center. Of course, someone obligingly carried the news to the town, and Canyon Center quailed. The Butcher had a ghastly record of killing men he wanted out of the way, without hesitation, of carving them up in a hideous fashion.

And the appalling thing was that no one in Canyon Center knew his face. That is, no one knew what man wore the alias of Butcher Krantz. The very next stranger you met on the street might be he. Most of the men who knew the Butcher as the Butcher—had died. He went his way, slashing and slaughtering, a figure of rising terror all along the frontier. Then he disappeared. True, he had rather formed a habit of disappearing after he had committed a killing, but he never stayed out of sight for long. He always popped up somewhere, to kill again.

For years now no definite rumor had come to Canyon Center. The fear of Butcher Krantz died down a little, and a few of the bolder citizens ventured to scoff at the predicted arrival and even at the existence of the Butcher.

Until one day they found the body of Big Hank Purdee in the lower ranges of the Saw Tooth Mountains. The skull was cleft in two and the body so slashed and mutilated that they knew it must be the work of the Butcher. The wise ones told tales of the slashed corpses found in Krantz's trail in California, and pointed out that the marks on Purdee's body were the same. The place was not much over a hundred miles from the old mining town. It was but a matter of days before he would reach Canyon Center. The scoffers were silent. A good many strapped on guns they had not worn for years.

The only other legend of the frontier of any importance was the legend of the Lost Cabin Mine. Oddly enough, no one had ever thought of connecting the two legends in any way. As for Butcher Krantz, in a country that was wild and lawless he was the wildest of any. In an era when ruler, judge and jury were embodied in a six shooter, he was too fast on the draw to be human. He was a menace to peace of mind, an ever present threat to life and security. A hundred men had said, at one time or another, that they were going to kill Butcher Krantz.

Several of them had tried it, with such disastrous results that no one had cared to attempt it again. The only man in Canyon Center who was not afraid of Butcher Krantz was Crook Alvord. Crook had come to Canyon Center some six years before, a short while after Butcher Krantz had last been heard from—though no one had chanced to suspect any connection between those two chronological events.

The weight and bloody horror of Butcher Krantz's reputation were evidenced by the circumstance that men could continue to fear him so long. For over six years he had remained out of sight, yet men lived in secret terror of his suddenly coming to light again, of his abrupt appearance in their midst. Some men in Canyon Center said it was queer that Crook Alvord wasn't afraid of Butcher Krantz. Others said that Crook Alvord wasn't afraid of anything.

They erred. He was afraid of his brother, Mark.

CHAPTER II
TWO OF THEM

CROOK hadn't seen Mark for a long time. He never wanted to see him again. He had no memories of Mark that were cherished, that were kindly or warming to the heart.

Mark Alvord was arresting to the eye. Not for

16

beauty. He was only moderately tall, barely six feet in height. He was lean as is a grizzly in spring. His long, narrow, lead-colored eyes had a hungry, predatory look. He was wide in the shoulders and big boned. His face was thin, sharp featured, smooth shaven, pinched. His too-large head was topped by a thin growth of drab-hued hair, and he had neither brows nor lashes—or at least they were so light in tone and growth that they failed to show. His tongue was ready and caustic, his temper dynamic, his spirit fearless and stubbornly per-sistent. And he hadn't a friend on earth.

He knew it, but he didn't know why. He lived openly and shot squarely, but no one ever drew close to him. Under the perfunctory cordiality of those with whom he associated he felt the chill of thinly veneered reserve. He pretended that he cared little, but the pretense was weak and he couldn't deceive himself.

For twenty-five years he had shifted from boom camp to boom camp—and quarreled with his brother Crook, though he longed passionately not to do so. There was a perverse devil in himself that he could not control, the existence of which made him antagonistic and surly towards all men. Even to Crook he was alien.

For years there had been a smoldering feud between the two brothers. A number of small grudges had piled up to a good amount of hard feeling. And yet there was something—blood, perhaps—which bound them together during their wanderings through the West. At last, riding out alone one day from the latest boom camp, Mark struck gold. Not a rich claim, but good enough to work for a while. He returned to town to have his samples assayed and passed the word on to Crook, who hit out to stake a claim alongside of Mark's strike. After Mark had wasted a good bit of time in the outfitting store and given Crook a long lead, he passed the news on to the crowd. With a whoop and a roar the temporary inhabitants of Taylor's Gulch headed for the hills, Mark in the lead.

Just before the new strike was reached there was a sudden ridge, and then a deep gully, through which the gold stream ran. There would be little warning for anyone working below of the approach of strangers. As Mark topped the ridge well in the lead of the crowd, he could see down into the gully where he had planted his stakes and where Crook was planting his. But the large, bent shadow that was Crook was not on the new claim, but fooling around on the parcel which Mark had staked out hardly twenty-four hours before.

A blind fury seized Mark. So Crook had switched stakes on him! Gratitude, huh! Crook was a cur, and he would lay into him for it. He rode up to Crook and accused him bluntly. He never stopped to ask whether Crook meant to hold his, Mark's, claim or not. He swore a great oath that if he ever saw Crook again he would kill him on sight.

Crook smiled a little and shrugged. He knew that he could match shots with Mark at any time and come out whole. So that was how much his brother trusted him! Couldn't even walk on his claim. Well, a dull stretch of panning gold would serve Mark right. As for him, this was as good a time as any to upstake and start out on his own. He had been hog-tied to Mark's temper long enough, and besides, he really had no desire to shoot it out with his brother.

Thus, in a blowup that came close to being murderous, the ways of the two brothers parted. Crook started out on that long trail which was eventually to bring him to Canyon Center.

Mark had wakened in the morning to find him gone. He had supposed Crook would brazen it out, as he had done so many times before. And then, only then, he noticed that the stakes had not been switched. His first thought was that Crook had been snooping around, after something else. And then, in self-reproach, he thought that Crook might have pulled out in anger at his brother's suspicions. Secretly appalled at the thought that Crook might really expect him to shoot on sight, appalled also at the prospect of working his diggings alone, he instituted a covert but frantic search for his vanished brother. It was utterly in vain. There was no trace to be found of Crook anywhere in California.

To Mark, any man who had journeyed beyond the confines of California had departed into the utter wilds. It wasn't conceivable to him that Crook could have left California.

He thought his brother must merely have taken hiding in some obscure part of the state. He thought also that Crook presently would get over his pique, that his anger would abate and he would come back. But time passed and continued to pass, and Crook did not return. Mark's thoughts and emotions underwent a change. His remorse over that last deadly quarrel began to wane. If Crook was going to act like that, let him! If Crook was fool enough to believe that Mark had meant it when he swore to kill him on sight, he was more of an ass than—but there Mark brought up short. Maybe Crook himself had meant it.

Mark suppressed a little shiver at the thought. That wasn't a pleasant idea to contemplate. For Mark was only a fair hand with a gun, but Crook was one of those men who could handle a gun so dexterously that any thought of trying to beat him to the draw simply seemed absurd. As Mark's remorse died, and he was reminded of Crook's uncanny skill with firearms, fear, anger and defiance began to grow in him simultaneously. Crook meant something by acting as he was doing. But whatever sly plan was in his head, he wasn't going to catch Mark napping.

Mark set himself to attain a skill with guns that

would lay Crook's mastery in the shade. Mark Alvord had one quality that, given a fair show, will make any man unbeatable: he had a dog-like pertinacity that couldn't say die, that didn't know there was any such word as quit and wouldn't believe it was licked even if it knew it. From that time forth Mark was so absorbed in acquiring gun skill that other considerations, such as worrying over Crook's nonreappearance, were relegated to the background, and time flashed by him unnoted. In two years Mark Alvord had acquired such a degree of proficiency that the most reckless gunslinger in the country was afraid to provoke him to the draw.

And still no sign of Crook. Mark grew restless, watching for him, listening for him, expecting to meet him at every bend in the trail. And now Mark's fear expanded till it outweighed everything else in his mind. He feared a hundred things, all rooted in Crook's unexplained absence, but mostly he feared Crook himself. He feared a dozen things that Crook might do, but most of all he acquired the rather fantastic fear that Crook might simply be waiting till Mark had given up all hope of his return, then suddenly pop up when he was least expected and catch Mark off guard.

Mark didn't intend to be caught napping there either. To circumvent any such intent on the part of his brother, Mark bought and raised a vicious Great Dane dog. He taught the dog to know him as master, to bear loyalty to him only, to hate all other men, and to kill at the prod of a word. He named the dog Satan. It became Satan's duty to watch at night as Mark himself watched in the day. Mark had become absolutely certain that Crook was executing some obscure and sly maneuver to catch him off guard.

When as a matter of fact it was simply that Crook *had* believed Mark meant it when Mark had said that he would kill him on sight. And Crook didn't choose to be shot by his own brother. He was as attached to Mark as Mark was to him, but Mark had never guessed it—any more than Crook had guessed the same hidden affection in Mark. They were two hard, gruff males, each pretending to despise sentiment, each inwardly desperately fond of and loyal to the other, and each mortally afraid to show any evidence of it. So Crook went away, and kept going and stayed away.

He was as different from Mark as a Guernsey bull is from a panther. He was not called Crook because of any inclination toward dishonesty but because of a crook in his spine. The deformity didn't prevent his being heavily muscled and unbelievably powerful. Had he been straight, he would doubtless have been taller than Mark. But the malformed spine had stunted him; he was scarcely five feet and seven inches in height.

He was rather simple and trusting of mind, rather gullible, and always ready to do something for somebody else. If others returned his friendly advance in kind, if he had a place to sleep and enough to eat, he was content, like a complacent good-humored bull in a clover field.

The only thing that marred life for Crook Alvord was the eternal fear that sometime Mark would find out where he was, would follow him, would come upon him when he least expected it and would kill him as he had threatened to do. None of the men in Canyon Center was aware that Crook lived in fear of his brother, or even that Crook had a brother. But they did think it strange that Crook had no fear of Butcher Krantz.

Once or twice some of the men had dared to speak about it. There were only seven men in the Happy Daze the afternoon Red Regan brought it up. Drinking had been desultory and Red Regan was leaning on the bar dawdling over a bottle of beer. Somebody made the remark that one of these days Butcher Krantz was going to pop up, he couldn't be very far away now.

"Yeah, of course he'll show up," agreed Red Regan, rolling a huge mouthful of beer over his tongue and swallowing it at a gulp. "If he got as far as where he hacked up Big Hank, he's going to keep on coming for here, like he said he would. Don't you think so, Crook, or is that why you ain't afraid of him? Or are you just sure that he's gone for good and ain't gonna show up again?"

"Oh, how the hell do I know?" Crook answered lightly. "How does anybody know anything about

Butcher Krantz? All I know is that as far as I'm concerned, there's things in this world to be a damn sight more feared of than Butcher Krantz."

"Oh, is *that* all you know?" Tom Peck inquired dryly.

The always good-humored Crook grinned. "Well, I do know that this damn town is gittin' duller every day. I wish Clawsuss would come in. About the only time we ever have any excitement in Canyon Center is when Clawsuss comes to town."

"Yeah," Regan agreed. "Ol' Clawsuss sure does liven things up a bit. Turns it into a regular spree every time he comes up, don't he? Funny fellow, that. I'd give my last dollar to know just what that geezer's idea is in shuttin' himself up that way."

"Sure!" jeered Peck. "You'n how many more? Every damn man in town'd like to know that."

"That ain't all they'd like to know about Clawsuss," Crook assured them with dry sarcasm. "But it's more'n anybody ever will know. I guess about half the men in this town'd die happy if they could know *where* Butcher Krantz is, and *who* Clawsuss is."

CHAPTER III
THE HERMIT
OF BUCKSHOT CANYON

THERE were numerous strange things about Clawsuss. Foremost, there was the fact that he chose to isolate himself in a rugged cleft in the mountains. To his right and to his left, from where his cabin stood on a narrow flat by the river's brim, sheer cliff-like hills rose, towering so high that a man must tilt his head to glimpse the clouds sailing over. A few hundred feet below the cabin the canyon described a sudden sharp turn, so that it gave the effect of a box. But above the canyon led straight away for a mile or more before it turned again. There the sky came down to meet the river and let in a little light. That was toward the west. Every night Clawsuss watched the sun set down the canyon walls.

For perhaps the area of an acre he kept cleared the strip of land above and below the cabin, and between him and the rushing river. There he grew potatoes and garden truck for his own use. When he wanted meat other than bacon and ham, he went out and killed a deer, or a young bear, or a brace of ptarmigan. All of them wandered by daily, less than a hundred yards away from his cabin.

The dark, shadow-blanketed canyon lay fifty-five miles from Canyon Center. Clawsuss was utterly alone. No territory near him for several miles in any direction gave the least hint of gold, and the surrounding country had long since been abandoned by experienced prospectors. Save for a few stray hunters and new gold seekers drifting by, he had guests no oftener than a half dozen times a year. And not much more frequently than that did he go into the town of Canyon Center.

Yet he was a familiar figure in what was left of the still wild, little, half deserted old boom town. Every man in Canyon Center knew Clawsuss of Buckshot Canyon, his dun-colored pack mules, Tom Sawyer and Bertha Brown, his small black pony, Nigg, and his huge brown gelding, Ripp. And as those men knew him, they knew, too, his isolated cabin. Hermit they called him, yet hermit he was not in the commonly accepted sense of the word. He evidenced no desire to avoid his fellow men. He was plainly delighted with every stray visitor, and he had a roaring good time of it every rare day he spent in Canyon Center.

Why he chose to remain in that hole in the hills no one knew. He was not prospecting. He apparently had enough money for his needs. He spent his time in his cabin, and other men often wondered what went on in that strange place where a man lived so rigidly to himself.

Another strange thing about Clawsuss was that in a land of heavy fisted, heavy swearing men he carried a single-shot pistol. But what he could do with that single-shot pistol and a handful of cartridges was legend in Canyon Center. Not even men phenomenally dexterous with a Frontier Model .45 cared to provoke that lightning. Clawsuss failed to broadcast the fact that night or day he carried under his armpit an ugly automatic which could spit a veritable stream of lead. He carried it against the hour the single-shot might need aid.

There was about him an eternal air of absent-mindedness, as though his thoughts were always far from his surroundings, on some important mission from which it was not to be lightly recalled. And though all men liked him, none ever drew close to him. The nearest he came to friendship was with Crook Alvord.

His size was incredible; newcomers refused to believe it until they had seen him. Six feet ten he stood in his stocking feet. He had a head like a bison, eyes like a hawk and a nose like a bloodhound. The head was covered with a shaggy mane of jet-black hair. The ears were large, and lay flat to the skull. The eyes were set deep under heavy brows that ran together in a beetling black ridge. He had a chest like a barrel and loins like a she-wolf gaunted with hunger. His arms were tough as hickory and his legs went them one better. Taken all and all, it was no exaggeration when Canyon Centerites stated that Clawsuss was a man.

If he had any name save Clawsuss, no one knew it. He himself might have forgotten it, so far as any disclosure of it could be ascertained. The "Clawsuss" he had acquired so many years previous that it had become part of him.

It had been fifteen years ago at least that the huge man with the black bison mane and agate-green eyes had walked into a saloon to get a drink. It was in another boom camp, and the giant prospector, as yet a total stranger to every inhabitant, had arrived with the last influx of miners. Leaning against the bar in the saloon was a dapper gambler with some education, a quick sense of observance and a share of ready wit. He looked up as the big man entered, and watched blank-eyed as the giant ordered and downed a prodigious glassful of raw whisky. When the huge stranger set the empty glass back upon the bar the gambler spoke impulsively, "Have one with me, Colossus."

The gigantic newcomer frowned, and his finger twitched as his hand dropped to the single-shot pistol at his belt. With cool significance he returned the gambler's gaze, a dangerous light in his eyes, and demanded curtly, "What was that name I heard you call me?"

"I called you Colossus," the gambler smiled. "It fits you. Certainly you're the biggest man I ever saw outside of a circus."

"What's Clawsuss mean?" the giant pursued, his frown unrelenting, his hand still at his belt.

"Why, man, don't you know what the Colossus was?" The gambler's feigned surprise piqued the mighty stranger's curiosity. He shook his bison-maned head, his hand wavering doubtfully away from the pistol as the gambler made brief explanation. "Why, the Colossus was a statue of the sun god, sometimes called Apollo. Old Greek stuff, you know. A sculptor named Chares made a statue of Helios a couple of thousand years ago. Put it up in Rhodes, near the harbor. The statue was said to have been over a hundred feet high. People used to say it originally stood with one foot on one side of the harbor and the other foot on the other side, so that the ships used to pass between its legs. It got thrown down and busted up by an earthquake, but the Colossus of Rhodes had become a tradition. It was one of the seven wonders of the world. Any time anybody wants to signify that a man's a whopper he can call him Colossus, you see. And I repeat, you're the biggest man I ever saw in my life!"

"Oh!" The black-bearded giant grinned and slapped the gambler jovially on the back, nearly knocking him off his feet. "That's a good one! Shore, I'll drink with yuh."

An hour later, in conversation with a miner in a nearby gulch, the giant calmly informed the stranger with whom he talked that he was "Clawsuss." The name stuck. The years rolled. The boom camps sprang up and died. Gold rushes came and went; while following in their wake a black-maned giant pursued the elusive goal that eternally evaded him, known to everybody merely as Clawsuss.

His cabin in Buckshot Canyon was as mysterious as he. It was built of logs designed like a fort and put together like a battleship. But it looked like a jail. It was no mere shed to serve as rain shelter and sleeping hollow. It was two stories high, though the second story held only a high, wide attic. On the lower floor were three large rooms. A bedroom, a living room, a kitchen and eating room combined, with a shed leanto built on its rear wall, for a storeroom. Clawsuss had planned and built the whole strange structure himself. It was slabbed inside and out with a shake roof to top it. The rooms were ceiled inside with slabs he had planed and chiseled and oiled; slabs ran from floor to ceiling. He had not removed the bark from the slab edges, and in between the slabs he had daubed the chinks with blue clay.

Very few pictures were on the walls, and only one of them notable. It was the largest picture in the living room and it stood out conspicuously against the mellowed tones of the old wood. It was a marine scene, brilliant with greens and blues, and a full rigged clipper ship was sailing head on into the foreground. A picture to claim instant attention anywhere, but more than notable here.

A queer enough house inside. Outside, save for

the garden, which was an ordinary enough vegetable patch, it was queerer still. Clawsuss had given his cabin a mansard roof. Stanch iron bars crossed the high narrow windows. Over the entrance of the building ran a wide deep porch, covered by wild climbing vines; cucumbers, old man, wild hops. Outside and inside the cabin had the grim aspect of a fortress—or a prison.

Across the roof of the porch, suspended from two iron swivels screwed into the eaves, hung a long strip of planed wood. On it Clawsuss had painted in bold black letters the name of his cabin and a seeming invitation to all intrepid passersby.

HELL'S GATE
Come A-Runnin

Men new to the territory usually paused when they had approached near enough to read that legend. Invariably they advanced to investigate the cabin and its strange owner, their minds ready for anything and their guns set for action. They went away with a bewildered memory of the giant Clawsuss, his agate-green eyes and booming voice, his garrulous hospitality and his air of sinister mystery. They seldom came back.

The coming of no man to that place was ever important until Mark Alvord stumbled upon that strange dwelling in the wilderness.

CHAPTER IV
OF HATE AND FEAR

MARK'S diligent search through years had finally won meager reward: he had heard from a drifting prospector that his brother Crook was somewhere in Oregon. He had packed a couple of mules with a supply of food, strapped on an extra gun, bought himself a horse and headed north. It might seem rather a wild goose chase. Oregon is a big state. But there was that stubborn determination of Mark's—and after he reached Oregon he asked every man he met if he knew where he could find Crook Alvord. Every man he met said no, and Mark continued doggedly on.

Cutting through the hills in the general direction of Canyon Center, his mules driven ahead, his Great Dane trotting at the horse's flank, Mark Alvord blundered into Buckshot Canyon and caught sight of the cabin with the mansard roof planted in the bottom far below. He stopped his horse, whistled in astonishment, and stared. What on earth was a cabin like that doing in such a Godforsaken place? He urged his horse and mules ahead, pushing on down the trail, his eyes scrutinizing the building through passing openings between boughs of surrounding trees.

As he wound ahead and drew closer he discovered the bars on the windows and became conscious of the atmosphere of the place. Again he drew his horse to a halt, frowning in puzzlement. Funny looking windows. Certainly it was a devil of a queer house and it must house a queer devil inside of it. Spurred on by his curiosity, Alvord again urged horse and mules down the trail till he drew close enough to read the sign. Then he threw back his head and laughed aloud.

"Well, I'll be damned! Hell's Gate!" He laughed again and turned to the huge dog squatting on its haunches a few feet away. He motioned toward the cabin, and issued a peremptory order to the Great Dane. "Satan, go up there and bang on the door. Doggone if we don't find out something about this ornamental jail."

The big dog rose and trotted ahead, took the four low steps at a leap and crossed the porch. Halting in front of the heavy door fortified with its powerful steel hinges, he raised one massive paw and struck the thick panel several taps. He stood listening with up-pricked ears, waiting rigidly at attention as he heard prompt answering footsteps inside. The door swung open.

Clawsuss stood before his guests. He glanced at Satan, then his gaze passed beyond to move swiftly over Mark, the horse and the mules. It came quickly back to linger admiringly on the mighty dog. The animal was enormous, of almost unbelievable height and breadth. His gray hide was slick and shining, his somber black eyes glowing continually with a dangerous shifting light. As Clawsuss stared at him, astonished at such gigantic size, the dog stared back, standing motionless. Then he suddenly reared to his hind legs, holding out one paw, and his slavering muzzle came well above Clawsuss' shoulder. Plainly the brute was offering open friendly advance, greeting the giant of Hell's Gate as he had been taught to greet other men. Gravely Clawsuss accepted the paw and shook it. The dog's tail wagged enthusiastically as he dropped to his fours, evidently satisfied, seated himself and looked up expectantly into Clawsuss' face.

"Well blast me if I ever saw the like of that before!" Mark exploded, staring in candid astonishment at the giant in the doorway. "What did you do to him—hypnotize him, or something? Why, man, that fellow's a frost-bit one hombre dog, let me tell you! I learned him to shake hands that-away, but he never does it unless I damned well make him. Ain't friendly."

"Shucks, that's nothin'!" Clawsuss boomed cordially. "I like dogs."

"Don't make a bit of difference if you do," Mark returned vigorously, swinging out of the saddle to the ground and stretching his legs with grateful relief. "Why, man—that dog's dangerous! He's *killed* three men; and he'd kill six more on the smallest excuse! But making up to a total stranger that way! He's never done that before in all his worthless life, and he's seven years old!"

"Well, now; is that so?" Clawsuss' eyes widened on the huge dog, then moved slowly to Mark's bony gaunt frame and pinched hungry face. Involuntarily Mark took a step toward the porch, paused straight and still, returning the giant's piercing gaze. A long, level, appraising look passed between the strange pair. Clawsuss said casually:

"Well, come in, stranger, and make yourself to home. This air out here always gives a man a appetite fit to bust a hoss. I was just gittin' my dinner. Fresh venison, fried spuds and green peas. Sound reasonable?"

"Sounds plumb enticing!" Mark replied lightly. The gaze broke.

Clawsuss advanced to the edge of the porch, the great dog following him, and Alvord turned to gesture toward the horse and burros.

"I just got off my horse, hoping you'd ask me in. Been covering a heap of country and I'm hungry as a bitch wolf with six pups. Wait till I tie this good-for-nothing jassack to a tree."

"Better unload the mules and take yore hoss down to the barn. Beyond the alders yonder." Clawsuss intervened, pointing to the log barn barely in view a hundred yards up the canyon, just below the sharp turn. "I'll wait here for yuh. I got supper on and kain't leave it."

Alvord nodded brisk assent and turned to slip the mules' pack. Silently Clawsuss stood and watched him, idly fondling the head of the mighty dog, as Mark turned the mules loose to roll and led the horse off toward the barn. When Mark returned a few moments later, Clawsuss was once more in the doorway, and the dog had seated himself by the huge owner of Hell's Gate. The Dane's long tail wagged contentedly, thumping the porch floor, as Alvord ascended the four steps and paused in front of the giant.

"My name's Alvord," he announced. "Mark Alvord. Brother to Crook Alvord, who I hear is somewhere in Oregon—and I'm lookin' for him. Maybe you're acquainted with the bullnecked galoot?"

Clawsuss repressed a start. Crook Alvord, the man he himself had come closest to calling friend for a good many years! And he remembered abruptly the veiled look of corroding fear he had sometimes surprised in Crook's eyes; the look he had seen most sharply evident when Crook had once remarked that so far as he was concerned there were worse things to fear than Butcher Krantz. But Crook had never said what it was he feared, or *who*. Could it be this unheralded brother, this man with the grim lead-gray eyes and the stubborn jaw? Something out of the ordinary was here, certainly. Plain for any ears to hear, when Mark had spoken Crook's name, there was an undertone of bitterness and venom in his voice.

Again Clawsuss measured him with a dissecting gaze: Mark returned the stare, unwinking, and in the look something passed between the two men much the same as had passed between Clawsuss and Satan. Silently Mark held out his hand. Clawsuss took it, and Mark's fingers were lost in the crushing grip of Clawsuss' mighty paw.

"If yuh kin beat that!" Clawsuss exclaimed. "Yeh, shore I know Crook—knowed him ever since he come to Canyon Center five, six years ago. Fine boy, Crook. So yo're his brother? Imagine that! Never knowed Crook had a brother. Can't say yuh favor him none in looks. Does he know yo're headed this way? He'll be plumb tickled to see yuh. But come in! Come in! Yo're welcome as a bar'l of Three-Star Hennessy! I'm Clawsuss."

"Colossus!" Mark started, stared slightly and grinned. "Well, I'll be eternally damned. Colossus! Man, you sure look it! Good name for a fella *your* size. Come to think of it, it's a *right* good name. Kind of grand sounding, ain't it?"

"Yuh think so?" Clawsuss returned the grin. "Never thought much how it sounded. Just come right in, Mark."

Alvord followed him across the threshold into the big living room of the cabin. The great dog, following, hung close to the giant's heels.

CHAPTER V
THE LINK IS FORGED

MARK glanced around the dusty cobweb-littered room. He turned as Clawsuss paused beside him in the center of the big room.

"Hiyu skookum place you got here in this hole, Clawsuss. Did you build it yourself? Kind of thought you did. Sure is an unusual house. But don't you ever get fed up with your same-old-stuff company away out here to hell and gone?"

"Nope." Clawsuss grinned again, and beckoned Alvord to follow him into the kitchen where thick slices of deer steak were broiling over the coals. The dog followed, wagged his tail and sat down at the giant's feet. Clawsuss tossed him a piece of meat and went on talking to his newly arrived guest. "Me and myself gits along pretty good. We can both drink enough to light up a dozen ord'nary sized hombres, we never lies to each other, and we don't fight." He held up the smoking meat. "How yuh like it, pardner? Rare?"

"Yeh. Blood runnin'," Mark returned, eyes on the steak.

No man had ever called him pardner before. But his eyes were without expression, and a silence fell over the two men as Mark watched Clawsuss return the venison to the coals.

Mark Alvord read men rather accurately. But this man he could not read. The giant's eyes were as clear and unveiled as green agate. There was nothing hidden about the man. It wasn't as if, in gazing into Clawsuss' eyes, he looked into an obscured spot, or an empty place. There was plenty written there, but it was written in an unknown tongue—as if it were inscribed in Arabic, and Mark Alvord couldn't read Arabic. If Butcher Krantz was a man of terror, Clawsuss of Buckshot Canyon was a man of mystery. But one thing Mark knew. The friendly welcome in Clawsuss' eyes was as genuine as it was unmistakable.

Mark spoke suddenly, frankly, "Well, Clawsuss, my pedigree ain't very much—but here it is. I been hitting the boom camps and drawing a deuce most of my life. I've panned enough dirt to build a mountain, trying to make a strike, asking nothing of any man and giving the same. Started out to— to settle a little affair with Crook, sighted your house from the top of the hill and come down to investigate. Ain't got no relatives but that Durham-faced Crook, less friends than that and no active enemies. Ain't got no more idea than a prairie dog where I'm going from here. I got to have a little session with Crook, seeing that's what I come for. Beyond that—I don't give a particular damn what I do or where I go after I pass on from Canyon Center."

"Yeh?" Clawsuss turned from the stove and fixed

Mark with a steady look. Clawsuss read men rather accurately, too. And he was remembering again that stark look of fear he had surprised in Crook Alvord's eyes. He was becoming momentarily more certain that that fear *did* have something to do with the advent of this brother, the brother Crook had never mentioned. He smiled, a slow smile that made Mark watch him intently. "I was just wonderin' what's the use of yore passin' on, Mark. One place is good as another when yo're huntin' gold. Better stick around this locality. Lots of gold in the gulches south and west. Yuh could make yore headquarters here. Ain't much fun travelin' alone. I been doin' that quite a spell, myself. Shore would like to have somebody to chaw with and see kin they drink faster and talk longer than me come evenin's. Reckon you'n me oughta git along right good. I got lots of room. Better think it over."

"Lord, man—*that* don't need no thinkin' over!" Mark's thin face glowed with a light that warmed his sallow skin and appeased his hungry eyes. "Me'n you and Satan ought to git along and no questions asked! Look at that worthless dog!"

Clawsuss turned to glance down at the huge Dane. The animal was crouched at his feet, watching his face with grave friendliness. Mark leaned forward in his chair, and his eyes darkened with excitement.

He raised his gaze to the giant's, meaningly, as he spoke, "I reckon that dog's got real sense,

Clawsuss. And ol' Satan's judgment is good enough for me! We stay. Damn glad to stay—till you order us to move on."

"Well, now! That's plumb white of yuh!" Clawsuss grinned his pleasure at the instantaneous decision. "Yuh'll be a long time goin' then. Come on over here and stick your feet under the table and fill your innards, Mark. Come on, Satan. Yo're in on this. Thought yuh said as how he was a one-man dog, Mark?"

"You bet he is!" Mark's eyes were on the dog's sleek dark head as he approached the table and slid into a seat. "He's been mine for seven years, but the ornery brute never really belonged to me. He don't like me any too well." Mark paused, his eyes deep with some inscrutable bitterness. No, even the dog hadn't liked him. "But he obeys me because he knows what he'd get plumb quick if he didn't. He tried to jump me once, and I winged him. He's behaved hisself since then."

"Yeh?" Clawsuss raised his heavy black brows inquiringly as he placed the plate of steaming deer steak on the table and took a seat opposite Mark.

"Yeh." Mark nodded, and his gaunt face lighted with a sudden thought. He spoke slowly. "But I guess now—I guess he's found his man." Again he looked the giant meaningly in the eyes. "And I ain't crossing him none."

"Yuh don't mean—" Clawsuss stared, hesitating, incredulous, his gaze flashing to the dog.

41

"That I'm giving him to you? What else would I mean? He's yours right now more than he ever was mine. Says so himself, so I got to agree with him. Take him and welcome, and if he ever gets funny with you beat the tar out of him. I'm a son of a gun if you ain't the best matched pair I ever seen, too!"

The dog looked steadily into the giant's face, as though he thoroughly understood the transaction and was desirous of expressing his unreserved approval.

"Say, now—that's plumb white of yuh!" Clawsuss stared at the big dog, overcome with the magnitude of such a lavish gift. He had told the truth in his first words to Mark Alvord, but he had been too conservative in statement. He more than liked dogs. He loved anything from a mongrel cur to a highbred hound. He strove to express something of his appreciation, difficultly, after his own fashion. "I—I shore will see that he's treated right."

Mark nodded, as though that went without saying, but he was not thinking of the dog. He had forgotten momentarily his brother Crook and the grim mission that had brought him blundering into Buckshot Canyon. An unbelievable thing had happened to the lone man in the gaunt shell. The thing he had hungered after all his life had come when he least expected it, when he had given up all hope for it, and had come without the extension of any least effort on his part.

Mark Alvord had found a friend.

CHAPTER VI
THE PLAY BEGINS

BY the time Mark Alvord had been in Buckshot Canyon for two days, the men had ratified their abruptly formed bond of partnership. Mark didn't know what a kindred spirit was. He had no idea what kind of thing had been born between him and Clawsuss. He only felt with an intuition as sure as his breath, that here at last was the pal to whom he would stick till hell froze; and that Clawsuss miraculously would do the same for him.

Clawsuss, for his part, sensed deeper, looked further. He did not know that the gift of friendship he had proffered Mark Alvord had bought that man, goods, body and soul. But he did know that in Mark destiny had brought to his door a man whom he could trust. And Clawsuss trusted but two other men—Crook Alvord, and Garner Blue, the old shoemaker down in Canyon Center. He had come to the unalterable conclusion by now that the thing Crook feared *was* Mark's coming. No man, unless he were an utter idiot, could have been in Mark's company this long and not realize that there was a dark and bitter score between the two brothers.

There was an ugly flare in Mark's eyes when Clawsuss brought Crook into the conversation. When Clawsuss reiterated heartily his statement that Crook would be tickled pink to see his brother, that brother veiled something furtive in his lead-gray gaze. And the giant of Buckshot Canyon deduced, and watched, and planned to thwart the purpose of that desperate gleam in Mark's eyes.

By the end of the two days Mark was refreshed from his long ride over the hills and gullies. Clawsuss, sitting with Mark before the roaring stove in the big room at evening, suggested that they go into Canyon Center the next day and surprise Crook. For a moment Mark sat motionless, his eyes on the stove. Then he nodded a quiet, nonchalant agreement. He spoke quickly, rather uneasily.

"Guess you don't have many visitors come popping in here, eh?" It was said at random, merely to break the silence, since his thoughts were becoming too uncomfortable to be borne with aplomb.

But it gave Clawsuss an opening. He seized it without hesitation. "Oh, fellas drift in every so often, Mark. Prospectin' or somethin'. Fellas new to the country who don't know they ain't any gold right around here. They see my cabin and amble down, same as you did." Clawsuss rubbed his hand absentmindedly over the head of the huge dog lying at his side, and his eyes were fixed on the flame-lit isinglass in the stove door. "Some of these days the fella I'm waitin' for will ramble in, and then there'll be somethin' doin'.'"

"Oh! That so?" Mark turned his head to look Clawsuss in the face, but he could see only the rugged outline of the grim-set profile, the bison-maned head bulking black and fantastic against the glow of the stove door. "So you *are* laying for somebody? I figured you was. Damned if I didn't. What's his handle?"

"Well, he's knowed as Butcher Krantz," Clawsuss said slowly. "Or was, afore he kind of dropped out of sight when too many men got to wantin' him right bad. Mean fella with a knife. 'Bout six inches shorter than me, and ten pounds or so heavier. Kind of beefy lookin'. Smooth shaved. Black eyes, and brown curly hair cut short in a stiff bristle. Had a blue scar zigzaggin' clear across his left cheek. Ugly fella—looked like an ape."

"Never seen nobody looking just like that," Mark returned. "Where you last run up again this galoot?"

"Californy." Clawsuss paused for a moment, thinking hard. "Southern Californy. 'Bout fifteen y'ars ago. Yuh ain't from Californy by any chance, Mark?"

"Best State in the Union, I hear," Mark said without enthusiasm. "Yeah, I been there. But I ain't *from* there. I'm from Texas, Arizony, Wyoming and Alaska."

"Gosh, now; yo're a man of parts!" Clawsuss

boomed admiringly. "So yuh never seed or heared of Butcher Krantz, eh? Huh. Thought possibly yuh would. Papers was full of him some y'ars back, pictures and everythin'. But he made a gitaway and kind of dropped out of sight, like. Well, reckon I'll make some coffee to guzzle on while we sits here and talks. It—it's a kind of long story—about Butcher Krantz."

Clawsuss rose from his chair and went into the kitchen. The dog followed him, yawning lazily, and Mark sat motionless in his chair, listening to the sounds that came from the other room, rattle of spoon and coffee can and granite pot. In the silence the fire in the stove crackled loudly. He felt an unaccountable sense of relief when Clawsuss returned to place the blackened pot on the stove, to set down a thin can of sugar alongside two cups, and resume his chair.

"Plumb has to have sugar," Clawsuss grinned. "Seems like I kin talk better when I got some perfect coffee to wet my gullet. D'yuh know what perfect coffee is, Mark?"

Mark raised politely inquiring brows. "Why, no, can't just say as I do."

"I read it in a book once," Clawsuss explained and there was an air about him as of a man who makes small talk deliberately, deferring some unavoidable thing he is reluctant to broach. "Some feller by the name of Tallyrand said it. He said perfect coffee was black as death, sweet as love, and hot as hell. I reckon this coffee is jist about it. Drink hearty and fortify yourself, Mark. This is gonna be a ugly story—too ugly to be told more'n once."

CHAPTER VII
THE OTHER TWO

THIS was the way of the beginnin', Mark," said Clawsuss. "Butcher Krantz killed a couple of fellas and messed 'em up pretty hideous with a knife. The hull town he was in went plumb crazy and started out to git him. But they never caught him at all. He sneaked north aways, and hid out till the rumpus kind of died down and he could make a clean git-away. The place he hid in was old and deserted, off by itself quite a little ways from the nearest town. Nobody'd lived there for y'ars. Not since the family that owned it broke up an' disappeared.

"The house was what was left of an old estate, and it was knowed as the old Symone house. There was some kind of crazy talk about the Symone fambly bein' cursed and nobody would go near the house or have nothin' tuh do with it. It jist stood there goin' tuh rot and ruin. Old man Symone had come to Californy to git rich quick. He hadn't got nothin'. The gold fever was in his blood, and he couldn't listen to jist settlin' down and workin' up slow-like.

"So he leaves the wife and kids and skins out to Alaska, shore sartin he'd make a strike there. The two kids was Norman and George. George was a pretty big kid when his dad went to Alaska, but Norman wa'n't only a baby. Symone stays away a few y'ars, strikes it big in Alaska and comes back rich. Sets his fambly up proper and builds this big house away off to itself like a king or somethin'.

"He's so plumb tickled with his good luck that he brings his wife a souvenir of the mine which set him on easy street. This souvenir ain't nothin' but a little half pint whisky flask chock full of nuggets —biggest nuggets he could find—none of 'em smaller'n a grain of corn. He's cut the initials of the mine's name on the cork of the flask. It was the Minnie Anne, named fer Mrs Symone.

"George and Norman was always standin' round lookin' pop-eyed at all them yaller nuggets, till old man Symone got skeered somebody'd steal 'em and he has a little safe cut inta the wall and hangs a picture over it, and tells the wife to keep her souvenir in there. Them nuggets plumb fascinates George, and he begs his mother to take 'em outa the safe and let him look at 'em purt' nigh every day. He sees 'em in his dreams. Old man's always tellin' about the gold fields up there, and the kids and the missus is always listenin' interested. George never gits tired hearin' about it. He's got a great imagination, and he gits plumb worked up over the gold fields.

"He can see the long hard days, pannin' and diggin' and hopin'. And he can see the wild whoopin' days when a man makes a big strike and the hull country races to stake out all the land around him. Time he's fourteen that kid's got the gold fever worse'n ary man ever had it. And it gits so hot-like in his blood that it knocks all sense out of him, and he ups and runs away to be a prospector and find a mine of his own. They never sees or hears of him agin.

"Then things started goin' wrong with the Symone fambly. That's how that fool talk of a curse got started. I guess it kind of busted Mrs Symone up to have George run off thataway. She jist kept gittin' peakeder, and peakeder, and finally she died. That hits the old man pretty hard. Then he loses all his money speculatin' in minin' stock. That hits him harder and he jist cain't stand it. He too lays down and dies.

"Then that talk of the family bein' cursed gits goin' around. People fights shy of Norman. He's a awful sensitive young fella, and it pizens his heart and makes him mad. He cain't even rent the big house, let alone sell it. So he lights out to be a prospector, too. And the old house stands there deserted and fallin' to pieces, for y'ars and y'ars.

"Then this Butcher Krantz does his killin', comes along and hides in the old house to lay low till he can make a clean getaway. While he's there he gits to rootin' round to see can he find any money. He finds that old safe in the wall behind the crayon picture and he busts it open. Ain't nothin' in it, only that whisky flask full of nuggets. But that's mighty interesting to him, at that.

"He's pretty smart, Mark, this Krantz fella is. He sneaks outa the country and heads north some more—keeps goin' till he comes to some more gold country. He ain't gonna cash in with that flask of nuggets, not in the reg'lar way. He's figured out how to plant them little gold seeds and make 'em grow inta a few thousand bucks. He salts a claim with 'em, pretends to be sick and offers to sell out.

"There's a coupla pardners prospectin' around thataway and he tells 'em about his claim. Says his name is Amos Krantz. The pards go to look the claim over. One of 'em is this George Symone that run away when he was a kid. He's prospected all over the country fer y'ars, bummin' around busted, still hopin' to make a strike. His pard's name is Cass Gregory, and he's a real pal. This Cass has saved up purt' nigh four thousand dollars. He's gonna use it for a stake to buy a good claim for him and George Symone, or find a real good claim and set up to work it out systematic. He figures Symone can pay back his share of the grubstake when they strike it rich.

"Well, these pards sees this claim of Amos Krantz's and falls fer it. Krantz has salted it pretty smart. Cass agrees to buy it and pay $3,500 cash. The pards moves into the dinky cabin Krantz has built, and Cass tells Krantz he'll git him the money immediate. Cass has it in town at the saloon—bartender keeps it in the safe for him. Cass leaves Symone at the claim and goes in to git the cash.

"While he's gone to town George Symone goes snoopin' around lookin' over the claim, pickin' up nuggets here and there. But these crooks allus slip up, Mark, no matter how smart they be. And Krantz was a smart one. Educated, well speakin'—didn't appear jist like a crook. But he slipped just the same. *It never occurred to him to bust up that flask and burn that cork.* He jist salted the nuggets and tossed the flask and cork aside in the bresh. George, rootin' around, finds that cork. Little way beyond he finds the flask.

"Now, George ain't forgot for one minute the flask of nuggets that started the gold fever in him. He knows instantly just what's happened. He goes on grim, pickin' up every nugget he can find and puttin' 'em back in the flask where they belong and where they been all them y'ars. But they's been scattered pretty well, and he only finds about half of 'em. He puts back inta the flask the black old cork with the M A cut in it. Then he goes back to the cabin to wait for Cass.

"Cass comes in and George tells him they been jist about to buy a salted claim. They're pretty mad, but they agree the best thing they can do is just say nothin'; pack up and git out. But afore they kin leave, this Krantz shows up and asks fer his money. Cass and George tells him where to git off. Krantz draws a gun on Cass and tells him to hand over the cash. Cass refuses. Krantz plugs him. Symone ain't got his gun on him, and Krantz is a lot quicker on the draw than Cass. He gits Cass plumb to rights. Symone goes hogwild and jumps for Krantz. Krantz shoots him, too. George Symone goes down like a ton of brick.

"Krantz goes over and rolls Cass to his back, frisks him and gits the money, counts it to be shore it's all there, and stuffs it in his pockets. Then he takes out the huntin' knife that's stuck in his belt. Now, George Symone had noticed that knife afore. It was kind of unusual lookin'. Pretty good-sized knife, it was, Mark, with a handle made of black wood. The end of the handle was made into a bear's head, and flat on top of the head Krantz had carved his initials. Yuh could see that A.K. when yuh was standin' six feet from the man, jist by glancin' down to his belt. Well, he yanks out that knife, leans over Cass, deliberate, and slashes up his face somethin' hideous. Symone is lyin' on his face, and this Krantz contents hisself with givin' him a few nasty swipes on the back of the head and neck. Then he goes out.

"Now, Symone's a kind of a husky cuss. All Krantz done was to knock him out and bleed him a little. He's lyin' there half conscious, knowin' all that's goin' on. Pretty soon he comes clear to, and he lays there and jist cusses the daylights outa everything. Then he sits up, kind of groggylike, and takes stock of things. There's Cass, dead and all cut up, and all the money Cass saved is gone. Symone gits up and moves around and feels hisself over a bit. Pretty well slopped up with blood he's lost and kind of weak from it. But he knows he ain't hurt so bad. By this time it's come evenin'. He sits there all night with his dead pard, swearin' he's gonna git Krantz if it's the last thing he ever does. Come mornin' he's feelin' pretty fair and he wraps Cass up in a blanket and goes out to bury him. Has to take it kinda slow, but he gits a hole started.

"And listen, Mark—when he's diggin' that hole he cuts right into a ledge of rotten conglomerate that's richer'n mince pie! He just sits there and stares. He's a kind of sentimental cuss, and he couldn't cash in on his mother's old souvenir. Plumb couldn't do it. And he'd been mad because he was so flat busted. But here he's got all the stake any man needs. Seemed like the Lord done put that gold in his hands so he could git out and hunt down this Amos Krantz.

"He waits a while till he gits to feelin' better agin, then he takes Cass and goes onto a little ridge overlookin' the gold strike, and buries Cass there so he kin kind of look down on the diggin's.

"Symone's kind of cut up and shot to pieces all right, but he's a tough hombre and couple of weeks sees him about as good as new. Then he gits busy.

Gits hisself a patent on the claim and works it clean. It sits him pretty nigh on easy street, too.

"Then he starts out to hunt down this Amos Krantz. He feels certain Krantz will be followin' the gold rushes where crooks git away with a lot of easy jack. So he goes on followin' 'em hisself. But he don't find hide nor hair of Krantz. For three years he trails from boom camp to boom camp like he's been doin' but he cain't find no trace of Krantz anywhar. Looks like a pretty hopeless business.

"Then George hears about this remark Krantz has made several times, about he don't know jist whar he's likely tuh go, but there's one place he knows he's goin' afore he kicks out, and that's tuh Canyon Center. So George comes tuh Canyon Center. He builds hisself a good house off a ways from the main town, and from the other prospectors' diggin's, and he sits down tuh wait till the Butcher gits ready tuh keep his word. He figured that was a better way tuh be shore of gittin' a chance at him than chasin' around lookin' for him and not knowin' whar he was. So—George sits down tuh wait. He—I been waitin' now, Mark, for seven y'ars."

A grim silence followed as Clawsuss' words ceased, a pregnant stillness that lengthened and gradually accrued more weight, till it became unbearable with two men's thoughts.

"Good Lord, man!" Mark broke into the silence at last, staring into Clawsuss' eyes with an awed sense of discovering a friend half mad. "You ain't kind of off in the head about it, seeing your pal killed and being cut up that way yourself, are you? Ain't one chance in a million he'll ever show up again."

"Mebby. I dunno. Begins to look like it." Clawsuss' dark face was shadowed with gloom. "But I'm still hopin'. I got this house all ready fer him if he comes."

"Yeh?" Mark's eyes narrowed, studying Clawsuss sharply. "I thought there was something funny about this house. Them bars to the windows. Pretty strong all the way round. Better'n a jail."

"Yeh—better'n a jail. Yuh said it." Clawsuss' booming voice was strange.

"Funny name you got for it, too—Hell's Gate."

"Yuh think so?" Clawsuss swung round his bison head and there was a sinister gleam in his eyes. "Well, Mark, when this guy Krantz goes outa the cabin after shootin' and cuttin' up the two pards, he ain't got no idee Symone is alive, half conscious, and can see and hear even if he cain't move yit. And he laughs, Krantz does; and he says out loud, ugly, 'Good-by fellas. I'll see you at Hell's Gate!' " Clawsuss straightened in his chair, his eyes ablaze and his face set in hard lines. "And here at Hell's Gate, the trap baited, I'm waitin' for him."

"Well, and if he does come? Then what?"

"Little settlement; that's all." Clawsuss relaxed in his chair, but his face kept its grimness. "I ain't treatin' him to no necktie party, nor I ain't fillin' him full of lead, nor I ain't turnin' him over to the Gov'ment. I'm jist keepin' him here in solit'ry confinement, like. Reckon that'll be plumb punishment enough for him, way I got it fixed. If he was left ramblin' he'd go on killin'. If the Gov'ment got him they'd hang him. I want him to have time to think. Huh—the coffee's bilin'!"

Clawsuss got up to remove the pot from the stove and pour the steaming liquid into the waiting cups. Mark's eyes followed him, puzzled. As Clawsuss filled the second cup, Mark exploded.

"But hell's fire and brimstone, man! Why ain't you bumping him off the minute he shows up, if he does? Why ain't you carving him up and giving him some of his own medicine?" Mark's lead-gray eyes sparkled fire with the heat of his indignation. "Them fellas don't suffer just sitting and thinking."

"That depends, I reckon." Clawsuss rose from pouring the coffee, standing straight to his enormous height, and his dark face paled as his eyes sought Mark's. "It depends on how they think and what they think about. Mebby I should have said on what they're made tuh think about—because I'll make him think all right, once I git him there. I've plumb got to." He hesitated a moment like a man come to the lees and dreading to drink. Then he added starkly: "Yuh see, Mark, it don't matter now, but I found out that this Krantz name was an alias. Butcher Krantz is—my own brother, Norman Symone. And a man don't kill his brother deliberate. That's kind of little, and cheap, and mean; and besides it's cheatin' on the Lord, who says vengeance is his'n."

Mark sat very still, and his own face went whiter than Clawsuss'. The Butcher was the giant's brother! And a man didn't kill his brother deliberate. Little, and cheap, and cheatin' on the Lord. And Mark thought of Crook, the brother *he* had sworn to kill on sight. Clawsuss' voice broke into the tense silence, level, weighted with some emotion that chilled Mark to the bone.

"The Lord says vengeance is his'n, and I ain't buttin' in on the Lord's business. I ain't wantin' to kill Butcher Krantz. If I could kind of herd him off to hisself and make him think and git some sense to his head, he might straighten up surprisin'. And I reckon we'd git along right good after a while."

"I—I reckon you may—be right," Mark admitted, uneasily, avoiding the giant's probing eyes. "I reckon I kind of agree with your sentiments, after all. Maybe he *will* come. Won't do no harm to hope, anyway."

"And to-morrow we goes in to see Crook," Clawsuss said quietly. "I reckon he'll be plumb tickled to see yuh."

"Maybe," Mark returned grimly. "Maybe I kin —maybe I better go in alone first when we get there. You and Satan can wait outside till I call you. I—I'd kind of like to have a word with Crook, uh—er—offhand, so to speak."

"Shore, all right." Clawsuss raised his coffee cup in his big hand. "Crook's a fair hand with a gun, ain't he?"

"Fair." Mark bit the word off as though he were afraid of it. "Little slower'n me."

CHAPTER VIII
ACCORDING TO THE GODS

SOME people hold that most of the upheavals and changes in the lives of men hinge upon chance. Others, who look deeper, and figure from the root of things, know that there is no such thing as chance.

Somewhere the omnipotent gods of destiny sit, on their obscure thrones, continually plotting, arranging, weaving, unraveling and rearranging; and nothing that they do is hastily or inadvisedly done. All that they ordain is for a purpose and works unalterably toward the materialization of their objective: so that some events which seem to smack of chance are merely deeply laid plots, plots so deeply laid that those whom they concern cannot read into them at all—until afterward.

Whatever particular god was in charge of Canyon Center and its inhabitants reached out a hand and set in motion a stream of events which was to change the lives of Mark Alvord and Clawsuss of Buckshot Canyon in a most unexpected way. And the stream had its source as far away as the drawing room of a fashionable house in Pittsburgh, Pennsylvania.

In this particular drawing room, at the particular moment in which Mark Alvord realized he had found a true friend in Clawsuss, Jo-Anne Blue was striding up and down, shouting words of bitter rebellion. Her mind was utterly wearied from incessant mulling over the unbearable situation in which she found herself. For years, ever since her mother had gotten her divorce from Garner Blue, they, her mother and she, had been doing things they didn't enjoy and associating with people they didn't like, all because her mother, now the important Pittsburgh matron, Mrs Luther Birdsall, had a mad passion to break into society. Jo-Anne's mind had passed over years of restriction, of pompous formality, that had been her life in the East. When her mother had divorced Garner Blue to marry the wealthy Luther Birdsall, she had been made the legal guardian of Jo-Anne. Confined in the gilded cage of the Birdsall mansion, the girl often thought of, though she could hardly remember, the cabin of Garner Blue in Canyon Center. There was freedom, there was the great expanse of hills and forests, there was some degree of happiness! Jo-Anne's eyes swept over the heavy appointments of the drawing room with an expression of disgust.

The elaborate mural on the wall, the marble statues and the huge cloisonné vase on its richly carved teakwood stand, the conservatory just beyond—all evidences of the Birdsall fortune.

At last she had found a reason to leave all this, to go back to the dimly remembered cabin of Garner Blue in Canyon City. For the past year her mother had been pushing her, thrusting her with devious nudges and innuendoes, into an engagement with the very eligible Victor Petridge, the steel man's son. And now Jo-Anne, faced with the realization of what this loveless marriage would be, had been telling her shocked mother that she was going to break the engagement.

Mrs Birdsall, lifting her gaze to meet the defiant light in Jo-Anne's eyes, spoke with asperity. "You must be mad! What will our friends say? And think of the scandal. Our social position *must* be maintained. Even your step-father's wealth and prestige will not be able to gloss over. How do you yourself intend to face people?"

"I don't. I'm going to visit my father until things quiet down."

This, to Mrs Birdsall, was a last straw. Garner Blue had abandoned even the mite of respectability his law practice had given him in the days in which she was married to him. Now he was a mere cobbler, a laborer who made shoes for prospectors and gamblers and cow hands. In Mrs Birdsall's shallow mind Jo-Anne's visit to Canyon

City would be the end of everything. Once her real father was known there would not be an eligible young man in Pittsburgh who would as much as look at her. Mrs Birdsall wearily continued her losing fight against this mad project of Jo-Anne's, but it was soon evident who would win.

As for Jo-Anne herself, she was constructing involuntarily a mind picture of the father she did not remember. She had a clear inner vision of a thin, bent, little white-haired old man stooping over a rough bench, driving tacks into great heavy boots.

The door into the hallway opened and Luther Birdsall appeared on the threshold. Jo-Anne heard the slight sound of his footsteps and turned her head. As her gaze rested on Luther's obese fatuous face, queer lights glowed in her eyes. Luther—with his millions and his idle days and his playing at being somebody. Luther—who could keep his smooth aplomb, and wrap Mrs Birdsall and her three sons in wool fleecing with complacent ideas of having done his whole duty. Luther had no place for her now. She was to be exiled to the west coast, to a little mining town and a dusty cobbler's shop. Her eyes blazed and she greeted him coolly.

"Good afternoon, Luther." How he hated having her call him Luther. It had always been his desire that she call him father, but she had never done so. She eyed him now with mock demureness.

"You've come just in time to bid me farewell. I'm taking the first train west upon which I can obtain accommodations. Will you miss me?"

"Hmmm. Going West? What's all this?" Luther quite missed the irony in her words. He crossed the room and paused by his wife. His gaze was still on Jo-Anne. "And when did we make this momentous decision? Miss you? Why certainly. Certainly, my dear child! Of course we shall miss you."

Luther was funny when he assumed his pompous dignity, Jo-Anne told herself. Very funny. "How decent of you!" She smiled sweetly, mockingly.

"I'm going out to Canyon Center and keep house for my father till this affair blows over. I think it very advisable."

"Well, well, now. Perhaps it is." Birdsall tilted his heavy face at her seriously. "That will be very nice. Very nice indeed. However, you must remember that keeping house for your father in a cobbler's shop will be somewhat different from the kind of life you have been used to here. It will not mean simply ordering the maids about and getting out of temper when the butler forgets something you told him to do in the morning. It will mean cooking meals with your own hands, washing dishes, doing your own laundry. I fancy it even might include scrubbing floors." He seemed a bit vague as to just what squalid duties might be entailed.

"How gallant of you to prepare me for the

worst!" Jo-Anne turned toward the door. "Nevertheless, Luther, since my father's cobbler shop is infinitely better than no place at all, I have decided to go."

CHAPTER IX
A REUNION

CANYON CENTER, Oregon, and hills, and sunset. At the edge of the little mining town, neatly squared off by a zigzag rail fence, a roomy one-story frame building stood on five acres of land. Around the building stretched two acres of garden, vegetables, flowers, wild shrubs and trees, growing pretty much as they desired to grow, so long as they grew. Squarely through the center of the acreage ran a wide clear creek shaded by tall balsam poplars. A gravel path wound from the front door of a time-mellowed and moss-chinked log cabin on the bank of the creek, through the garden to the rear door of the frame building. Across the front windows of the frame building was painted a sign in heavy black block print:

GARNER BLUE
SHOEMAKING & REPAIRING

The sun was making a valiant effort to dispel the clouds riding boisterously across the sky, and for a moment won its way, making a brilliant spot like a sun dog in the middle of the western arc, squarely before the open door of the shop. Inside the shop Blue was busily halfsoling a shoe. He heard a slight noise, like a light step, and raised his eyes to the front of the shop. His gaze halted, riveted on the open door.

A woman stood there, framed by that bright spot in the sky, a young woman. Blue recognized her instantly, for, although he had not seen her for fifteen years, he had often seen her picture in the papers he bought to keep track of her. It was entirely possible that he might have recognized her had he seen no pictures of her anywhere, she was so like him. She had the same high-arched brows, the same deep eyes, the same straight nose and firm mouth; even the small squared chin was a feminine replica of his own.

Garner Blue stood very still. His only daughter. After fifteen years, his daughter. What could have brought her here? She had never even answered his few lonely notes, before he had grown discouraged and stopped writing. He had no possible way of knowing that she had never received them. Mrs Luther Birdsall had considered it very unwise indeed to allow any tie to be fostered between Blue and the young girl, ever since she had been separated from her husband after seven years of marriage. Let closed scores stay closed, had been Mrs Birdsall's idea of the matter. What Garner Blue thought and felt had ceased to trouble her. But the loss of his children had never ceased to trouble *him,* and his love for his daughter had been the strongest love he had known. Behind him, clinging to his trouser leg, stood little Petey, the boy of a neighbor who had died. Blue had adopted Petey, happy that in some small way he could replace his lost daughter. Now Blue stood gazing at her, at a loss to account for her presence, not knowing how to break the silence of fifteen years.

She stood as motionless as he, returning his wondering gaze. Their thoughts were very much alike. Her father. After fifteen years—her father. Into her mind flashed an absurd and frivolous phrase—"what is wrong with this picture?" It was not the picture she had conjured back there in Luther's house, a thin little white-haired man bending over a rough bench. The man who stood facing her, so like herself that she knew him instantly for her father, was tall and upright and brilliant. His head was held high with the continual poise and pride of a man secure in the serene knowledge that he has kept faith with himself. His thick black hair was untouched by a strand of white. The strong face, molded into lines and planes of humor and tolerance, was unmarred by the lines etched by the vicious stylus of dissipation.

So they stood, staring and astounded, facing each other suddenly out of the years, in the grip of a silence neither could break. Petey broke it for them. "Grandfer, who's the pretty lady?"

Garner Blue laughed. "You're very welcome, Jo-Anne. You see, I read all about your trouble in the papers. Petey, you must call this lady Mother," that was Garner Blue's way of acknowledging his daughter.

Blue stepped forward to unlatch the little gate separating the waiting room from the work shop. The ice was broken. Before he could continue to say anything else, Jo-Anne literally rushed toward him. Blue swung wide the gate and caught her in both arms. In the next instant she was sobbing on his shoulder, rather wildly, and Petey was standing off a pace, staring at them with wondering and puzzled eyes.

Blue held his daughter tightly for a moment in silence, then he pushed her back from him and scrutinized her face intently.

"What's it all about?" he asked quietly.

Somehow she blurted it all out in a rush of bitter words. "And they hadn't any room for me back there," she finished. "So I came out here to wish myself on you till it all blew over."

For a moment Blue gazed at her with a queer unreadable expression in his eyes. Then he nodded, as if he had reached some secret conclusion he had no intention of divulging for the present, and he smiled at her so warmly that she felt as if she had come from storm into harbor.

"Well, you certainly came to the right place," he said lightly, deliberately relegating her uneasiness and bitterness to the background as if such small affairs as what the Birdsalls might think, or any of their kind, were small considerations in his life and hers. "There's always room for you where the old man is. But you must be tired. It's a long way out here from Pittsburgh. You come on over to the house, and you can rest while I rustle you something to eat."

All eyes and ears, Petey followed Jo-Anne and her father through the back room, where Blue kept his supplies, through the rear door and down the gravel path. Jo-Anne's eyes took in the scene with a hunger she did not understand. The vegetables were beginning to yield up their first green fruits. The beds of flowers were showing heads everywhere, and numerous early ones were already a gamut of color. The moss-roofed cabin was splotched with pink where a wild vine, clambering over it, was beginning to shower into bloom.

Behind the cabin, bulking huge and mysterious in the near distance, reared a mountain. The sun shone upon its face, bringing into relief against the tree-clothed slopes the raw red earth of mine workings, seams in the mountainside that sprayed outward like seams in a miner's wrinkled hand. The sheering peak of the mountain reared against a sky as sunset-red as hammered bronze. Beneath the bronze-tipped peak, a thin veil of mist floated, like a lavender scarf thrown carelessly so that it unfurled across the mountainside. Spreading away from the nearer mountain serried ranks of blue and lavender hills and peaks seemed to stretch on into eternity, growing fainter till they merged into all space.

Slightly to the left, against the sunset sky, a lone eagle poised black and solitary on motionless pinions, homing to his eyrie somewhere high on the rugged peak.

Jo-Anne caught her breath.

"What's the matter?" Blue asked quickly.

The girl gave him a sober smile. "I never dreamed it could be as beautiful as this."

"You won't find it so beautiful inside the cabin, I fear," Blue said dubiously. He stepped forward and threw open the cabin door. "After what you've been used to back there—"

Jo-Anne looked through the open door. Inside, the chinks between the logs had been plastered with blue clay and moss. The bare unpainted floor was scrubbed white and clean, over the windows hung curtains made of flour sacks washed till the lettering upon them was faded into a mere shadow. At the far end of the room hung pots and pans in an orderly and sedate row behind a neatly polished wood-burning range. At either end of the room doors opened onto the adjoining bedrooms. A great black bearskin rug was stretched upon one wall, and a great fireplace made of carefully chosen cobblestones added the last touch that meant home to Garner Blue. Jo-Anne turned upon him.

"You dare apologize for a place like this?"

Blue smiled. "Well, it doesn't seem possible that you could help being influenced by the combination of gold fronts and green backs."

"I paid a large price to get here," Jo-Anne said irrelevantly. "But it was worth it."

CHAPTER X
METAMORPHOSIS

THREE weeks can make or mar a lifetime. In three weeks Jo-Anne had changed the world for Garner Blue. From the back of his shop she looted a mail order catalogue. She gave the cabin a thorough inspection, then sat down to fill out a mail order blank. Later, numerous boxes and bundles arrived at the cabin, and Jo-Anne gave herself the treat of engaging in sundry tasks she had never performed before. She painted the floors silver-green. She laid upon the floors thick rugs of silver-green, gold, blue and rose. She replaced the flour sacks with lacy curtain stuffs of dull blue, with little rose-colored flowers running around the border. She took the bearskin rug down from the wall and laid it in front of the fireplace. She painted the old kitchen chairs silver-green. And she had a hilarious time doing it all.

Then her interest expanded, beyond the cabin and the little cycle of life there. To the town and its surroundings and the men who inhabited it. She took Petey by the hand and walked down the one main street of the town, unafraid because hers was not a timorous spirit, undaunted because Blue told her that she and Petey were as safe in Canyon Center as they would be in Luther's house—safer, as a matter of fact. Jo-Anne was fascinated by the quaint old wooden buildings and deserted cabins. Men in rough mining garb turned to look at the slender girl and the golden-haired child, and nearly every man they saw had a word of greeting for them. As they approached the Happy Daze saloon Crook Alvord strolled across the slanting porch and stood leaning against one of the rough pillars as girl and child drew abreast.

"Good mornin', Miss," Crook addressed Jo-Anne genially, friendly eagerness in his eyes. "Lookin' the town over? You're Garner Blue's daughter, ain't you?"

"I am." Jo-Anne smiled. "And you're Crook Alvord, I know—because my father was telling me about you. Dad thinks you're just about right, Crook."

Crook's eyes widened. "Oh, that so? Well, he sure is a fine fellow himself, isn't he, Petey?"

"I like you," said Petey unexpectedly. And some strange instinct prevented him from asking, as many a child might ask, what made Crook walk that way.

Crook's florid face flushed with pleasure. "Do you, now? Well, I sure like kids. Ain't many of 'em around this town. Would you mind if I gave him somethin', Miss Blue?"

"Not at all." Jo-Anne smiled down at Petey and up at Crook. "Little boys always like to have things given to them. But I don't like being called Miss Blue, Crook. It always makes me feel so strange. I think you'd better just say Jo-Anne."

Crook's ruddy face flushed again. "Sure. Sure! I can see one thing, Miss Bl—I mean Jo-Anne. You're real home folks. We was kinda afraid you might be—well, you might—" Crook stumbled and floundered, embarrassed, at a loss for tactful words.

Jo-Anne laughed, but there was understanding in her twinkling eyes. "I know what you thought, Crook. You thought I'd be stuck up, with an elevated nose and no chin. No, not me. I don't like that kind of thing any better than you do. I've been living among a lot of people like that, but it didn't take. I suspect I must be like my dad."

Crook nodded emphatically. "I'd say! You even look like him."

"Was you going to give me something?" Petey put in anxiously.

Both Crook and Jo-Anne laughed, and Crook said he'd go right and get it. He disappeared into the saloon, to return almost instantly, hands over-flowing with his gift. He filled Petey's eager reaching fingers with golden-brown pretzels and crystal-clear rock candy, neither of which Petey had ever seen before.

Crook grinned, highly pleased at Petey's exclamations of wonder and delight, and turned to glance over his shoulder at the sound of footsteps emerging from the saloon behind him.

A man who towered above Crook, a man wearing heavy miner's boots, overalls and a flannel shirt, advanced toward Crook with a small slender man in tow. The big man spoke in a booming baritone voice.

"What you tryin' to do, Crook? Steal a march on all us guys and keep Petey and his new ma all to yourself?"

Crook grinned, and winked at Jo-Anne. "Well, you fellows inside could hear all that was bein' said."

"Yeah," assented the big miner. "That's why we come out. If Miss Jo-Anne wants to feel at home we reckoned as how she might like to meet some of Canyon Center's real important citizens."

Crook chuckled. "This here is Single-Shot Andy, Jo-Anne. The little fellow is Shy Bolcom. These two galoots, along with six other fellows, has been prospectin' around in this country for God knows how long, and they're still hopeful. Canyon Center calls 'em Single-Shot's gang."

"Gee, ain't he big?" Petey demanded of Jo-Anne, admiring eyes on Single-Shot Andy, mouth full of pretzel.

"Oh, I ain't in it, son," Single-Shot assured the child. "You wait till you and your ma see Clawsuss."

"My father told me about him, too," Jo-Anne put in. "I thought Dad was exaggerating. Why, he said the man was almost seven feet tall."

"He is," Crook confirmed. "Lives away above here in Buckshot Canyon. He's a moose of a man. Your dad wasn't exaggeratin' none. Huh, here comes Horse-Pistol Mike and the rest of The Gang."

Jo-Anne wandered back to the shoe shop nearly three hours later, to recount to Blue her and Petey's adventures. They had gone for a walk, Crook Alvord had stopped them and they had met most of the population of Canyon Center. They had met Single-Shot Andy, and the rest of his gang, Shy Bolcom, Horse-Pistol Mike, Link Parker, Yellow-jacket Bevans, Windy Lucas and Spade Lowry. Highway Bill she hadn't met, he was out watching the diggings for Single-Shot and the rest of the gang. But she had met numerous others, and she had heard so much about Clawsuss of Buckshot Canyon that her curiosity was fully aroused concerning the man.

"But it seems to me there's something very inconsistent here," she told Blue, frowning, puzzled. "Those rough looking men, the kind of men popularly supposed to be dangerous, are the kindliest men I have ever seen. The way they treated Petey you'd think they had never seen a child before, and that poor deformed Crook Alvord is as gentle as a lamb."

Blue chuckled. "He would be around you and Petey. But no man who has any respect for his life is going to provoke Crook Alvord. And Single-Shot Andy, so they say, never shoots but once—because he doesn't need to. But—I'd rather trust my daughter and her future to the hands of Single-Shot Andy than to the hands of Luther Birdsall. How did you like the boys?"

"Who wouldn't like them?" Jo-Anne countered. "Petey's in love with the whole Gang, and I think I am too. Yellowjacket invited us to come out and see the diggings. Would it be all right for us to go?"

"Certainly, if you want to." Blue nodded emphatically. "You'd be as safe as you would in your own back yard, and I'll bet you'd have a good time. What did you tell Yellowjacket?"

Jo-Anne grinned at him. "I thought they looked like a darned nice Gang, so I told him Petey and I would come up to-morrow. He and Single-Shot Andy are coming for us early in the morning."

"You look as if you were really beginning to enjoy life out in this neck of the woods," Blue remarked slowly.

"Beginning!" Jo-Anne echoed. "Why, I loved it from the minute I came. I feel like a different person."

But she did not realize how different. Neither of them had the slightest idea how far reaching were the changes working in them and around them, ever more swiftly, nor how terrific were the issues being born, the tempests rising to thunder about their heads. They are merciful gods who decree that the future shall be hidden from man till he meets it face to face.

CHAPTER XI
JO-ANNE SEES BENEATH THE SURFACE

EARLY in the morning Single-Shot Andy and Yellowjacket Bevans drew up before the shoe shop with an extra horse for Jo-Anne. Single-Shot took Petey up on the saddle ahead of him, and the three rode on to join the others of The Gang, en route to the diggings. The wiry horse Single-Shot had brought Jo-Anne was about as different from the sleek mounts owned by Luther as one horse can be from another, but she learned him easily and sat him without discomfort.

Single-Shot wanted to know what she thought of Canyon Center by this time, and Jo-Anne told him that she was enormously pleased with it, and ravenously curious about Clawsuss, of Buckshot Canyon.

"Is that all the name the man has, Single-Shot?" she asked. "Doesn't any one ever call him Bill or George or Dick, or anything of the sort?"

"Not as I know of, ma'am." Single-Shot turned to Link Parker. "You ever hear anybody call him anything else, Link?" Link shook his head in silent negation, and Single-Shot turned back to Jo-Anne. "I guess that's all the name anybody knows for him, ma'am. Queer soundin' all right, ain't it?"

"Why, it can't be his real name, you know. Did you think it was?" Jo-Anne raised her eyebrows in frank surprise. "It's plainly a fictitious name, Andy."

Single-Shot Andy scowled in puzzlement. "Why can't it be his real name? Guess I don't get that word fictitious."

"A name that isn't your own, that you are using merely to keep people from finding out what your own is, Single-Shot," Jo-Anne explained. "And it can't be his own simply because it is clearly a distortion of the name Colossus."

"Colossus what?" Yellowjacket wanted to know.

"Just Colossus, Yellowjacket; about the biggest statue you'd ever want to see. People use the name now to epitomize anything very huge. Somebody has given the name to your giant of Buckshot Canyon because of his size, and he's kept the name because he wanted an alias, and maybe it tickled his fancy. The more I hear about that man the more I wonder about him. I'm eager to see him. Does he come to town often?"

"Oh, just as happens to suit his fancy. Sometimes he's showin' up every coupla weeks or so for a few months, and then again we won't see him for three or four months. I invited him out to see our diggin's but he ain't never come yet."

Jo-Anne wanted to know where the diggings were, and all The Gang started to explain at once. The Gang had hung together for years, trying to make a strike. It was Single-Shot Andy who had found the spot at last that promised to repay them adequately for their faith and unbegrudged labor.

"I'd been prospectin' up Saw Tooth Canyon, along Red Dog Creek, when I found it," Single-Shot explained, with the sudden loquacity of a man come upon the subject close to his heart. "See them jiggy-jagged mountains off over there, Jo-Anne?" The big miner pointed to a rugged range bulking clear and green-brown in the near distance. "Well, them's the Saw Tooths, where Red Dog Creek heads. Ain't much of a creek till it hits Saw Tooth Canyon, then it gits purty big and comes down there rarin' to beat hell. Tharabouts where we found the body of Big Hank Purdee. It flattens out considerable as it goes through Pete's Narrows 'n settles down to Blister Valley. About forty mile back in the Saw Tooth Range, jest above the Narrows and Blister Valley, I come onta this find."

"Some find too, it was," Horse-Pistol Mike put in, determined to have a word or two to say.

"Yeah, it sure was," agreed Single-Shot emphatically. " 'Tain't a big canyon, where we are. 'Bout a mile long and a hundred yards wide. One side rises up about a hundred feet. T'other side runs from fifty to a hundred in height. At the far end the canyon narrows down to 'bout thirty feet across an' from fifty to seventy feet deep. They's a ledge of rock there that God Almighty musta planned for the abutments of a dam. Leastways, that's what we used it for. We've got plenty of elevation. Everything we need. We dammed Red Dog, put up our hydraulic giant and got busy. We ain't got so much done yet, but by the time we git all the alluvial soil in that quarter section run through our sluiceways we can buy the hull town of Canyon Center and six more like it."

"Now you're getting ahead of me, Single-Shot," Jo-Anne interrupted. "*What* is alluvial soil? And who was Hank Purdee?"

Single-Shot grinned. "It's soil that's been put there by water, ma'am. Washed away from one place and left in another. And they's plenty gold in the alluvial soil in our canyon. Never you mind Hank Purdee, ma'am. That name jest slipped over my tongue. Too ugly story fer you to hear."

Single-Shot went on to describe the canyon and

its claims, as the horses left Canyon Center behind them and came to the rolling lower hills leading up to the Saw Tooth Range. They camped that night on the bank of Red Dog Creek, below Blister Valley, and in the morning resumed their journey, to reach the site of the diggings well toward noon.

Just before they arrived at the diggings, which were still hidden from view by a bend in the canyon walls, they passed within view of a tall man working in a peculiarly listless fashion, swinging his pick as if he cared little whether he ever loosed any gold-bearing earth and rock or not. He barely glanced up at them as they passed, but something in his wide staring eyes gave Jo-Anne a feeling of uneasiness and chill.

"Whoever *is* that man?" she asked Single-Shot when they had gone beyond hearing of the lone miner. "The way you spoke to him, he can't be one of your Gang."

"No ma'am, he ain't." Single-Shot frowned, and shifted Petey to an easier position on the saddle. Petey had been excited and interested all the way, but he was growing tired and rather impatient to reach the diggings where he could move about and play to his heart's content. Single-Shot Andy glanced back at the man in question, then looked sharply at Jo-Anne. "He's a fella you feel kinda sorry for, ma'am, and yet you kind of feel pretty much like lettin' him alone."

"Damn sure I'm gonna let him good and well

alone!" Horse-Pistol Mike made his declaration with a great deal of feeling. "I ain't lost nothin' around that guy. I don't like the way he looks at a fella."

"Well, maybe you wouldn't look any too happy about it if you was in the fix he is," Link Parker observed charitably.

"What's the matter with him?" Jo-Anne asked quickly. "Is he ill?"

"In a way of speakin'," Single-Shot admitted. "In the head."

But there they arrived in sight of the diggings, and Petey's shouts of delight and Jo-Anne's own high interest in the whole scene quite drove the strange and solitary man from their thoughts and conversation.

For three days the girl and the wildly happy child made the Canyon alive with their presence and their excited exclamations. They viewed the dam, pride of The Gang, rearing to a majestic height across the canyon. They stood for hours watching the roaring Red Dog rush through the hydraulic giant, beating the alluvial soil through the sluiceways, washing out the gold for which the Gang toiled. Single-Shot Andy gave Jo-Anne a large piece of rose quartz, and Yellowjacket gave her the biggest nugget he had mined. Petey crowed over a smaller piece of rose quartz, and shouted aloud when Shy Bolcom lifted him and allowed him to dip his hand in the foaming sluice.

All in all they had a royal stay, and both of them were rebellious at having to leave their genial hosts and the group of pole cabins when it was time to return to Canyon Center. Single-Shot Andy accompanied them, to see them safe to the edge of town. They left the diggings proud possessors of all the gifts and souvenirs they could carry, with hearty invitations to come again ringing in their ears. Jo-Anne sighed as they rounded the bend in the canyon which shut the mine workings from sight.

"Oh dear, Single-Shot. I certainly hate to go. Don't you, Petey?"

"You bet. But we can come again, Mother. Can't we? Can't we come again?"

"Why, yes. Maybe. If I stay here long enough. He's certainly had the time of his life, Andy." Jo-Anne frowned and fell silent, as her gaze encountered the solitary miner who had attracted her attention on their way up the canyon. "Oh, there's your queer man who's sick in the head, Single-Shot. I'd like to get a good look at that fellow. What would he do if we rode close enough to speak to him?"

"Nothin', ma'am. Jest look at you and ask crazy questions, like as not."

"But what's the matter with him, Andy?"

"He's lost his memory, ma'am." Single-Shot Andy lowered his voice, as they neared the man who had aroused Jo-Anne's curiosity. "He used to live in California, and somebody down there hit him a crack on the head with a rock. He woke up in the cabin of some fella that was takin' care of him, but he couldn't remember nothin' that had happened before. He—but we better wait till we git past him; he can hear what we're sayin' now if we don't watch out." The lone miner had ceased from his desultory labors, noting that they were coming his way, and was watching them intently with his wide strange eyes. "Howdy!" Single-Shot addressed him, as they came abreast and halted their horses.

Jo-Anne's eyes swept covertly over the man who pushed back his hat and stood for a moment surveying them in utter silence. His once well-fleshed body had shrunk to a state of emaciation which must have changed its every line from what it once had been. His face was gaunt and drained of color. His dark brown hair was drawn back in a sweep of shining waves. Over the left temple a patch of white hair stood out conspicuously against the brown. He looked first at Single-Shot, then at Jo-Anne.

"Howdy do," he said tardily to Single-Shot. He fixed his strange, rather wild eyes on Jo-Anne, and spoke civilly enough, yet with an oddly intense and restrained tone that made a chill run along her spine. "Do you know a big fellow named George?" he asked abruptly. "You ever see anybody have a whisky flask full of nuggets?" Jo-Anne shook her head in speechless negation, and he shrugged, scowled, and looked away, muttering to himself. "Makes people think I'm a damned idiot, I guess. Why should I care? Only way I'll find out is to ask."

Single-Shot Andy urged his horse into motion, and Jo-Anne only too gladly prodded her own mount, relieved that Petey had not seen fit to burst forth with any ill-timed queries. Once they were beyond earshot of the man, she turned to Single-Shot with a flood of questions.

"Heavens, what a wild looking thing he is! What does he mean, Andy? Why go about asking everybody such questions? Or does he ask them of everyone he meets?"

"Yeah, everybody." Single-Shot Andy nodded, his face brooding, his eyes sober. "You see, the only things he can remember is a big man named George, and that fantastic whisky flask full of nuggets. He can't remember the man's face, just that he was a whale of a big man and his name was George. He don't know who had the flask full of nuggets, but he says he can see it plain in his mind's eye. When he woke up in some fella's cabin, he knew who he was by some letters or somethin' in his pockets, and he remembered them two things. Everything else was as blank as mud. So he's been trampin' from town to town, tryin' to find a big man named George and somebody with a whisky flask full of nuggets."

"A big man named George," Jo-Anne repeated.

"A *big* man. Queer nobody has referred him to this man in Buckshot Canyon, this Clawsuss who hides his identity behind such an obvious alias."

"Somebody *did* tell him about Clawsuss, ma'am," said Single-Shot Andy grimly. "That's what he's doin' in this neck of the woods. He asked them questions of his of somebody south of here, somebody who'd heard of Clawsuss evidently, but who hadn't seen him. Whoever it was told him that there was a whale of a fella here around Canyon Center somewhere but they didn't know whether his name was George or not. He come along and asked us. We knew he was lookin' Clawsuss up, but we—well, we kind of—"

"You made excuses to keep him from going any farther," said Jo-Anne, with sudden divination. "But why? You can't keep him here always? He's bound to go on and see the man sometime? What's your idea, Andy?"

Single-Shot frowned, and shifted Petey against his chest. "Well, ma'am, I reckon as how we'd a little rather he run into Clawsuss when the rest of us is around to kind of keep an eye open. That's why I asked Clawsuss to come out and see our diggin's."

"But *why,* Andy?" Jo-Anne persisted. "I don't see why. I should think your man Clawsuss could certainly take care of himself. And this poor fellow, repelling as he is, isn't much more than a shell of a man."

"A pretty tough shell of a man, ma'am." Single-Shot's tone was grim again, and a little hard. "He's one of them tricky kind. He may be lyin'. Again, he may be tellin' the truth, and it might be purty bad business for this George if he finds him and knows him. Everybody likes Clawsuss, just as they likes Crook Alvord, and we ain't hankerin' to see no trouble stirred up for either of 'em."

"What's the man's name?" Jo-Anne glanced back over her shoulder, to discover that the solitary miner was standing unmoved, staring after them. She shivered and averted her gaze.

"Sure is a creepy cuss, ain't he?" Single-Shot had noted her glance and the involuntary shiver that sent a quiver across her shoulders. "Says his name's Norman Symone. Kind of high-fallutin' ain't it? Well, he can wait to see Clawsuss when Clawsuss comes out here. You see, ma'am, we don't *know* that Clawsuss' name *ain't* George—and we don't like the look in Mr Norman Symone's eyes."

CHAPTER XII

ONE MAN'S TERROR

AT the edge of the town of Canyon Center, Single-Shot Andy bade Jo-Anne good-by, placed Petey on the saddle in front of her and turned back to Saw Tooth Canyon. She rode down the street with her mind absorbed by the man with the wild haunted eyes, so absorbed in her speculations that she was unaware of any other's immediate presence till her horse came to a halt and Petey crowed a delighted greeting.

Jo-Anne lifted her abstracted gaze to see Crook Alvord standing almost at her mount's shoulder, one hand on the reins, one hand extending upward toward Petey a generous helping of rock candy. The girl smiled indulgently.

"Crook, you'll have him utterly spoiled. He never had so much attention in his life as he's had since I came to Canyon Center."

Crook grinned. "I reckon it won't hurt him none, Jo-Anne. Kids need some spoilin' before they git too big. If they wait too long some of 'em never git spoiled at all—and that's bad. How'd you like the boys' diggin's? They show you a good time?"

"They certainly did!" Jo-Anne was very emphatic about that. "And it was a novel experience for me. I'd never seen anything like it before."

"And big Andy, he gave me a pink rock!" announced Petey, fishing in his pocket for a piece of rose quartz.

"He'd a give you the camp if you'd asked for it," Crook assured him, a broad smile on his heavy florid face. Suddenly the man with the warped back raised a penetrating gaze to the girl. "What happened out there that kind of worries you, Jo-Anne? You look—almost scared."

"I suspect I am," Jo-Anne told him soberly. "At least, I saw a man I don't care to see again. A queer half mad thing who's prospecting there in the canyon below The Gang's camp. He's from California, and he's going around hunting somebody of whom he remembers only one name. He was hit on the head with a rock, and it left him that way."

"From California!" Crook had gone rigid, his hand gripping the rein till the knuckles showed white against the florid skin. The color receded from his face like an ebbing wave, and his voice was harsh with sudden hoarseness. "God'lmighty! And hit on the head. He—you say he's kind of blank in the mind?"

Jo-Anne stared, amazed at the reaction manifest in Crook Alvord. His attitude was one of consternation and stark terror. There flashed through her head the reminder that "Crook" was only a nickname; she had no way of knowing that Crook's name was not George. Dumb, literally tongue-tied with dismay, she sat her horse and stared at him. She'd come to like Crook whole-heartedly herself, and she knew now how Single-Shot felt about not stirring up trouble for Clawsuss.

"Go on," Crook commanded, in that strained hoarse tone that wasn't like him at all. "What does he remember? What's he look like? What's the name of the man he's lookin' for?"

Jo-Anne forced herself to speech. She spoke

almost as harshly as he, because she was frightened and bewildered, and because she was forcing herself to coherency.

"He doesn't remember anything but a big man named George. Oh! A *big* man!" Crook couldn't be called a big man. Jo-Anne caught her breath in a little flash of relief and rushed on. "And a whisky flask full of nuggets. He's rather tall, and very gaunt, with a queer long face and wavy dark brown hair—there's a white patch in it over one temple. His name is Norman Symone."

Crook drew a long, long breath, and exhaled it slowly, as if he had been holding his breath for an eternity. The slow color flooded back into his face, and fine little beads of perspiration stood out against the ruddy skin of upper lip and forehead. "Never heard of *him* before. God'lmighty, but that's a relief. Phew! You had me—you had me kind of lookin' at my hole card, Jo-Anne."

"Yes," said Jo-Anne meekly, and she wondered what man on earth could so inspire the dangerous Crook Alvord with fear. Then there flashed into her mind her father's version of one of the legends of the town. "I know. Crook! You were afraid he might be this Butcher Krantz!"

"*What! Me* afraid of Butcher Krantz?" Crook laughed, a bit unsteadily, still shaken with his relief from stress. "No, I ain't worryin' any about the Butcher, Jo-Anne. I—" He paused and looked intently into the girl's face. All humor faded from his countenance, and his eyes grew bright and stone hard, and she saw for a moment the man to be feared within the warped and twisted shell of Crook Alvord. "I ain't never told a livin' soul," he said slowly. "But somehow, I don't mind tellin' you, and I guess I don't have to ask you not to repeat it. There's only one thing on this old ball of dirt that I'm afraid of, Jo-Anne. My brother."

"Why are you afraid of your brother?" Petey asked suddenly.

Crook started. He had quite forgotten the child. Jo-Anne looked at him with startled and warning eyes, and he abruptly reached to lift the child from the saddle. "Oh, I was just jokin', Petey. I ain't really got any brother. You trot on inside and ask Pete Cobalt for some pretzels. He's got the same name you have, and he sure thinks you're just about right. Tell him I said to give you lots of 'em."

Instantly forgetting all about Crook's funny way of making a joke, Petey obediently trotted into the saloon to ask the owner for a handful of pretzels.

Crook stepped close to the horse, and lowered his voice, his gaze intently holding Jo-Anne's. "I haven't seen him for years, Jo-Anne. My brother. I—we used to quarrel, bad—awful! We had such a hot old argument one night that we threatened to kill each other on sight next time we met. I didn't mean it—I was just mad and I said it because Mark did. He *did* mean it. He's the kind that would. I—I just got up and left the country."

Jo-Anne shuddered. "He must be a terrible man, Crook. To hold a grudge against anybody like you."

"He ain't terrible!" Crook refuted, in instant and passionate defense. "He's a damn fine man, and I always liked him a lot, though I was kind of ashamed to let him find it out—he's so queer and drawn into himself always. Don't git the wrong idea, Jo-Anne. I ain't afraid of Mark because he's bad. I'm afraid of him because he's so damn good."

Again Jo-Anne stared. She stared at Crook for a long moment, then she slowly shook her head. "Because he's so *good!*"

"Yeah. He's so good I'd be turnin' in my grave if he ever come to grief through me. He's just kind of bitter inside, because he's so queer-like and solitary he couldn't never make no friends. That ain't good for nobody, Jo-Anne. And it hurts him, and he's got the impulse to hit back, you see. If he ever finds me, he'll kill me on sight just because he said he would. Then he'll be sick to the backbone all his life because of what he done, hangin' or nothin' else could ever make him suffer for it like he'd suffer just rememberin'."

"But Crook!" Jo-Anne interrupted. "You—from what I hear of you, you could just about beat any man living to the draw, as they put it. Couldn't you—stop him, some way?"

"No ma'am." Crook stared earnestly into her face, and his eyes were dark with distress. "You see, he's kind of slow with a gun, Jo-Anne. I wouldn't dare even touch mine—it'd be plumb murder. I know I wouldn't. If he ever come—I'd just have to stand there and let him shoot. And he'd live in dumb misery all his life because of what he done. And that's what I'm afraid of." Crook finished rather lamely, and Jo-Anne tried to find something to say, but before she could find it Petey came running back.

Crook swung the child up to the saddle in conspicuous relief at any opportunity to change the subject. "Well, well. Did you git all the pretzels you could eat? You'll turn into a pretzel yet, young man."

Petey giggled, and Jo-Anne found her tongue on forced, banal words. "He'll be getting fat as a pig, that's what he'll do. Well, we simply have to move along, Crook. Thanks for being so nice to Petey. We'll be seeing you again in a day or two."

But as she rode down the street, idly answering Petey's cascade of queries, she saw before her eyes the appalling look of stark terror on Crook's face. That a man could be so afraid of meeting his own brother! Plainly, Crook had buried himself here in the little corner of the world called Canyon Center, buried himself so effectively that his unnamed brother could never trace him. But the brother must be a man of dogged determination, from what Crook had said and hinted. And Jo-Anne suddenly found herself praying passionately that Crook Alvord's brother should never come.

CHAPTER XIII
A SHOEMAKER'S ALL

THAT night Jo-Anne and her father sat late in the cabin on the bank of the creek, after Petey had been put to bed, discussing her trip up the canyon with the boy, the strange man they had seen in the canyon, and the mystery of the man's numbed brain. She did not mention the grim fear that rode Crook Alvord.

Unexpectedly Blue glanced deep into his daughter's eyes. "You're really having a good time here, aren't you, Jo-Anne?"

"Heavenly!" The girl smiled. "I never knew there could be such a grand place and such real and interesting people. I know now that in Pittsburgh I was never able to recognize a healthy impulse or a sane and normal emotion. It was a terrible life."

"I'm sure that it was." Garner Blue nodded, a strange abstracted look on his face.

The next day Jo-Anne received a little letter from her mother. It was a missive redolent of relief and pleased gratification. The whole disagreeable affair had blown over, she assured Jo-Anne with some effusion. She could come back anytime now and she would be received back to the old set with open arms. It was even very likely that Victor also would receive her with open arms, and conduct himself as if nothing had ever happened, so long as nothing of the kind occurred again: which both she and Jo-Anne knew, of course, was a foregone conclusion. She enclosed Luther's check for a thousand dollars to cover expenses for Jo-Anne, and she would be expected home immediately.

With the letter in her hand, Jo-Anne left the cabin and walked through the garden toward the shop. She saw Petey paddling in the creek a short way down the bank. As she entered the room back of the shop she heard the drone of the electric finisher die down and cease. She crossed the back room and stopped in the doorway connecting the back room with the shop.

Garner Blue was bent over the lasting jack, hand-stitching a heavy sole. In his right hand he held a small instrument with a wooden handle. At one end the handle was flattened to fit the palm, for stabbing force. At the other end of the handle a long steel ferrule was set around a strong pointed tine. On the edge of the top-like handle was a triangular piece of shoemaker's wax adhering, black and distinct, like a mark.

As Blue pulled and tightened his threads, he became conscious of Jo-Anne's gaze upon him, and he lifted his eyes to see her standing there in the doorway. Without a word she drew close to him and extended the letter she had just received, which Crook Alvord had got at the Post Office and delivered to her. Blue laid upon a shelf the small instrument, stuck his needle into the sole he was mending, and took the letter from his daughter's hands.

He read it through, handed it back to her without comment, picked up the little stabbing instrument and bent over the lasting jack. His face did not change, save that it lost color. He said quietly, without emotion:

"I see. When do you go?"

Outside, in the garden, Jo-Anne heard Petey's shout. Luther Birdsall had what he wanted. Mrs Birdsall had what she wanted, her social position, safe at last. And she had safety for herself. All of them back there, they had what they wanted. But Blue—

She saw him as he would be after she would be gone, sitting bereft and alone in the cabin she had beautified, cooking and eating all his own meals, alone. Nights would be silent in the cabin that had echoed Garner's talk and he would have to bear the silence alone. She heard clearly the echo of his words—"Only once will I merit anybody's pity." Something like a hard lump came in her throat and her eyes stung. She swallowed. Through the stillness of the little shop, pungent with the odor of freshly tanned leather, her voice rose—softly, lest it break.

"Dad—I'm not going."

Blue straightened, rigid. He dropped his needle

and stood staring at her. Then his lips moved. "By God!" It was half oath and half prayer.

Jo-Anne winked back tears, and smiled at him. "But I hardly know how to write it, how to—"

Blue reached again for the letter. "You needn't. I'll answer that!"

Five days later the butler entered the drawing room in the Birdsall home and tendered to his mistress a small package on a tray. Mrs Birdsall received it curiously, glanced at the butler's departing back, and turned to her son Harrison, who had just come in.

"I wonder what this is. Why—it's from Oregon —it's from your fa—Mr Blue!" As she started to unwrap the package, Luther entered the room. She looked up at him with a puzzled frown. "I've just received something from Mr Blue, Luther. Well, what on earth!"

Harrison and Luther bent over to look at the small instrument which fell into her lap. It had a wooden handle, flattened at one end to fit the palm, for stabbing force. At the other end of the handle a long steel ferrule was set around a strong pointed tine. On the edge of the top-like handle was a triangular piece of shoemaker's wax adhering, black and distinct, like a mark.

Wrapped around the handle was a piece of paper. Mrs Birdsall removed it, and from within it there fell Luther's check to Jo-Anne for a thousand dollars. On the small piece of paper that had been wrapped around the handle of the instrument was written a single sentence.

"You asked for this so I send it by return mail."

"Why, I never did! I never asked him for anything!" Mrs Birdsall denied indignantly. "Harrison, what *is* this thing?" She pointed to the little instrument.

Harrison shook his head. But Luther leaned over her shoulder.

"Wait a minute, Gwen. I can tell you. I can tell you two things. One of them is that your daughter is not coming back. The other—is that." He laid a finger on the instrument in her lap. "By jove!" His voice held a grudging note of admiration. "The fellow's clever, at that. The instrument, my dear, is a shoemaker's awl."

And that was the evening Jo-Anne and Petey went over to take half of a cake to Crook Alvord, because Jo-Anne had baked it and was proud of her new prowess, and because Crook had a great fondness for cake and seldom could get any.

It was the evening that Blue realized to the full that his life was not to be empty and dreary again, for five days had passed and Jo-Anne had never wavered from her decision.

It was also the evening that Clawsuss, in his cabin in Buckshot Canyon, said to Mark Alvord:

"And to-morrow we goes in to see Crook."

CHAPTER XIV
FASTEST ON THE DRAW

IT was hot afternoon, and Crook was leaning over the bar, watching the boys crowd around the wheel, the tables and the faro bank. A couple of them had made a small strike westward in the mountains and had come in with a poke of gold dust to liven up the town. Somebody had just made the remark that the old burgh hadn't been so active for weeks. Crook shrugged, and complained that things were too tame altogether to be good for his system: a man grew plumb poison mean from doing nothing.

"God, I wish Clawsuss would come to town," Crook finished his comments fervently. "He ain't been in for a dog's age. He—holy cripes!"

Crook's voice chopped off on the violent oath, rising to such a note as no man in the room had ever heard in Crook's voice before. Startled, a half dozen men or more whirled to look. Crook stood half crouched, rigid and transfixed behind the bar, his face the color of unbleached linen, his eyes wide with horror, his mouth half open in consternation, his gaze riveted on the open swing doors.

A stranger stood there in the doorway, a lean tall man with long, narrow, lead-colored eyes. He was staring straight at Crook, and his thin sharp-featured face was as pasty as Crook's own. But what turned every man breathless was the fact that in either hand the stranger held a leveled gun, the weapons so leveled as to cover Crook and the other men in the saloon beyond him.

For a flashing moment every miner in the room was swept by bewilderment at the sight of Crook Alvord so paralyzed with terror; Crook, who hadn't ever been afraid of Butcher Krantz. Crook gulped and swallowed, and drew his mouth together difficultly and slowly, as if it were the most tremendous task he had ever attempted.

"Sit tight, everybody!" The voice issued from Crook's lips, but to the men listening in incredulity and dismay, it was not Crook's voice. It was the same hoarse tone Jo-Anne had heard when she spoke of the man from California. And the words Crook added were as unbelievable as that tone of stark terror. "It's me he's after, none of you."

"Yeh, sit tight," approved the man in the doorway. He stepped into the room, and the swing doors closed behind him. He advanced slowly toward the bar, and by now Crook's habitually florid face had attained a pasty sickly yellow. The man with the guns looked fully as ghastly. He had eyes for no one but Crook. It was to Crook he spoke. "God Almighty, don't look like that, Crook! I ain't going to shoot. I just wanted to get the drop on you, to stop you before you took a crack at me.

I got something to say to you. You willing to listen to me, Crook?"

The men crowding back against the wall, curiously watching the strange tableau before them, saw Crook's face flood with swift color then go white again. They saw his hands tremble, clamped over the edge of the bar. They heard the same hoarse harsh voice answering the stranger.

"Yeh, sure I'll listen. You've got me cold. I've got to listen, ain't I? What the hell you got to say?"

The other man's eyes went bleak. He hadn't wanted Clawsuss to know just how violent had been the quarrel between him and Crook, how deadly the oath he and Crook had sworn against each other. And Clawsuss stood just outside the door, beyond sight of any man in the saloon, waiting for Mark's word to enter. The lean man with the gun set his jaws squarely. The only way to avoid being little or mean or cheating was to come clean all the way. A man had to sponge the slate thoroughly once it was fouled. Mark's voice was cold and steady with repression, as he replied.

"Crook—we're brothers. We ain't got a soul in the world but each other. We swore to kill each other on sight, but I didn't mean it. Not even when I said it. I been findin' that blood is pretty thick after all. I want us to be done with all that quarrelin'. I want to forget it, and I want you to forget it. Don't you reckon that we might learn to kinda hang together?"

Profound silence hung over the room as Mark's voice ceased. Crook opened his lips and tried to speak, but no words would come. A little quiver ran along Mark's jaw, like a tic in a muscle, and a little white circle grew around his mouth.

"*Can't* you forget it, Crook? Can't we start clean? Say something, man. Say something! Does she go?"

"As she lays!" Crook's face again flooded with color, and this time the color did not fade again. He straightened, squared his warped shoulders, and started around the bar, hand extended, eyes glowing. "As she lays! Put up the irons, you skinny yellow-faced son of a sea cook. Put up the irons and shake on it!"

"Fair enough!" Mark returned, as though he and Crook had met after an amicable parting but a day old. But something stung his throat. He had read his brother's eyes. He holstered his revolvers and gripped Crook's hand, wrung it and grinned back, and no one saw the look that passed between them.

Each knew the other had meant what he said. The feud was at an end. If those strange two had anything at all in common it was the fact that the word of each was as sacred as an oath on a Bible.

"What does I owe the honor of this visit to?" Crook asked slowly, sober again. "I reckon you might as well spill it, Mark. You can't tell me you come all this way up here just to get on good terms with your only living relative. What's your game?"

"I ain't got no game," Mark denied, returning his brother's gaze unflinching, but his mouth went a trifle grim. For a moment he hesitated, visioning Clawsuss out there listening to every word. Well— clean slate! Mark went on, spacing his words distinctly, as though he wanted Crook to be certain of distinguishing every word. But that careful enunciation was for Clawsuss.

"I come up here to kill you, Crook, like I said I'd do, and not for another damn thing. I been run ragged for seven years—afraid you'd sneak up on me when I wasn't on the lookout. I bought me a brute of a dog and raised him to kill—to protect me from any little surprise visit you might be cooking up. Then I heard of you up here, and I bought another gun, and started for you. But before I reached Canyon Center I—I got me a pal. And he kind of changed my ideas. I give him the dog, and we come on in together."

"Ain't got religion, have you?" Crook jeered, to hide the emotion that surged through him and lit his pale eyes.

"Nope." Mark grinned, understanding, and his grip tightened for a split second as he dropped his brother's hand. "Damned if I ain't just got some sense! Well—my pal and his dog is waiting outside to come in."

"Well, for Pete's sake bring him in!" Crook roared jovially. "Bring him in! Any pal of yours is sure gonna find the door open where I am. Where's the dog?"

"Out there. Satan!" Mark turned to face the door. "You'n Clawsuss come on in here."

Clawsuss! Another concerted gasp swept the spellbound men who stood looking on. Crook's unknown brother showing up and claiming the mysterious lone wolf as friend! Before they had time to recover from the surprise of the last few moments and from Mark's amazing statement, Clawsuss strode through the door with the mighty dog at his side. The giant went straight to Mark, oblivious of every one else, and stopped in front of him, gazing intently into the lead-gray eyes.

"Shake, Mark!" Clawsuss held out a huge paw. "I knowed when it come down to scratch yuh'd be a plumb man. Shake!" He gripped the eager hand Mark thrust out to meet his and turned to the big dog. "Satan, stand up and shake with this fella here." He gestured to the open-mouthed Crook. "Yuh gotta like this fella, Satan. *He's* a plumb man, too."

Satan reared to his hind feet and proffered his paw. Gingerly Crook shook the paw, drawing back and eyeing the huge animal doubtfully as Satan dropped to his fours.

"By Glory, Mark! That's some dog. I'll bet he *is* a devil, what?"

"Devil from hell," Mark admitted pridefully. "Kill any man Clawsuss or me'd sic him on. Come on up, boys." Mark turned to address the trans-fixed onlookers. "You're all drinking on me. Celebrating the family reunion!"

"My brother, gents!" Crook gestured toward Mark, and turned to slip behind the bar. "Does you give him the glad hand?" The men broke from their stupefied trance, crowding up along the bar by Mark and Clawsuss, giving the Great Dane a wide berth, as they proffered royal welcome to the stranger. Crook beamed on them. "Have a snort of my special brand of liquid fire, gents. Guaranteed not to rust your hair, shed your skin or curl your toes. It's rat pizen and gun fodder, and it'll warm the innards of any man what's been froze for any-thing less'n six hundred years. How much'll you have, Mark?"

"Two licks and a barrel, and anything you got left." Mark leaned up to the bar, and grinned down at the dog seated at Clawsuss' feet and staring up at him unblinkingly. "Here's the old devil begging for his customary snootful. Give him a glass of beer with a finger of whisky in it, Crook."

"Sure. You bet!"

Crook slammed bottles and glasses on the bar for the men and began mixing the drink for the dog. He leaned to pour it into a small basin sitting on the floor back of the bar, and Mark interposed hastily, "No, just give the hound the glass, Crook." Crook stared, but started obediently around the bar, and Mark interposed again. "No, no, Crook.

Just set it on the bar." Crook obeyed, and Mark turned to the dog. "All right, boy, come and get it."

The dog reared to his hind feet and placed his forelegs on the bar. He bent his huge head, opened his great jaws and clamped them over the mouth of the glass. Then with one swift movement he upended the glass, demonstrating the facility which comes from much practice, turned the liquor down his throat and gulped it at a single swallow. After which he dropped the glass back to the bar, got down to his fours, and seated himself again at Clawsuss' feet, licking his chops and wagging his tail.

"Son of a gun, if he ain't a smart one!" Clawsuss boomed admiringly. "I've heared tell of dogs drinkin' thataway, but I never seen one do it afore."

"He likes his whisky straight," Mark explained, with pardonable pride in Satan's sophistication, "but you hadn't better let him have it none. He's too mean when he's drunk. Well, bale her in, fellas. Liquor up! The roof's off!" Mark lifted his own glass. "Here's mud in your eye!"

"You—you *staying* with Clawsuss?" Crook asked.

"He shore is!" Clawsuss affirmed vehemently. "Yuh wanta come out and call on us frequent, Crook. Why, hello there, Regan! How's the world treatin' yuh?"

"Oh, nothin' extry, Clawsuss." Red Regan set

down his whisky glass and ran a hand through his stiff mat of red hair. "Pay's kind of running out on my claim. Guess I'll have to shift along up the gulch and find me a better location. Peck says he saw some promising color over White Horse way."

"Don't know as it'd pay you worth the trouble, Regan," Peck himself spoke up from the other end of the bar. "Kind of skimpy lookin'. Tell you what, Red, I got a letter from Joe Calthorpe, down to Robber's Roost, 'bout a hundred miles south, and he says a fella made a whackin' big strike down there. Says it looks like another rush. Might look into it."

"Oh, you hear a lot about these rushes always comin' up. I don't put much stock in 'em." Regan shook his head doubtfully. "I kinda like it here. Some of these days somebody'll make another strike around here. I'm hangin' on an' waitin' for that."

"Well, you're waitin' for nothin' then," Peck grinned. "Never be no more big strikes around here, Red, unless somebody should happen to find the Lost Canyon."

"What lost canyon is that?" Mark put in, interested.

"I'll tell yuh 'bout it, after a while," Clawsuss promised. "I now rises to suggest that all hands around gives our undivided attention to the business of the hour. Crook, ladle out some more of that rat pizen of yourn."

"Yeh." Regan grinned and winked at Peck. "We ought to rip the old town up this evenin' and set her to goin' right."

Peck smiled broadly. The idea appealed to his sense of joviality. "Yeh, that's right," he agreed. "We hain't had any real excitement around here for God knows how long."

"But you don't want to get too hilarious about it," warned Crook. "Jo-Anne's kind of took to all of us, and gives us credit for not bein' too wild and woolly. I don't want you galoots to go and spoil it all by makin' plumb monkeys of yourselves."

Clawsuss glanced at Crook in quick surprise, and deep in his eyes a twinkle grew. "And who the hell is Jo-Anne, Crook?" he inquired. "Yuh ain't got a lady friend hid in this Gawd-fersaken hole, have yuh?"

"You're damn right she's my friend!" retorted Crook stoutly. "And she's Garner Blue's daughter."

"The hell!" ejaculated Clawsuss. "When's all this happen?"

"Why, she come out quite a little while ago," Crook explained. "Come out from the East to live with Blue. Fine lookin' girl she is, too. 'Bout twenty year old I guess. She's took to Garner Blue's boy, Petey—brings him around everywhere with her. Jo-Anne's kind of hankerin' to meet you, Clawsuss. She's heard so much about you. She's come to Canyon Center to stay, so you'll be seein' her sooner or later."

"Well, now, if that ain't good news!" Clawsuss beamed in appreciation of what the presence of a young girl undoubtedly would mean to Canyon Center. "Blue'll be plumb tickled. Now I recollect that I've heered him speak of havin' a daughter. Does she like the town?"

"Yes sir, she sure does," Crook assured him. "And she thinks the boys is all ace high, don't she, Andy?"

Single-Shot Andy, in town with Shy Bolcom to purchase provisions for The Gang, looked up from where he leaned on the bar, and chuckled. "She shore does, all right, Crook. She likes you best, though. Yo're a lucky cuss." Andy's bronzed face sobered. "The only fellow in this neck of the woods that she don't like is that poor fella who's prospectin' up in our canyon. That fella named Symone." He glanced covertly at Clawsuss, wondering if that name would strike fire.

A little silence fell, a silence queerly breathless. Into it the voice of Clawsuss crashed harshly. *"What did yuh say that fella's name is?"* Mark Alvord felt the giant grow rigid and still at his elbow.

The men crowded at the bar stared into Clawsuss' face, glanced at each other, and a flare of excited interest flew from eye to eye. Was Clawsuss, lone wolf of mystery, about to let them catch a glimpse of his shrouded past? Single-Shot Andy answered quietly, watching the giant's reaction to his words, "Why, his name's Norman Symone, Clawsuss. I feel kinda sorry for the poor fella. He must a been a danged tough hombre once, but I reckon he won't never be again. Got cracked on the head—lost his memory. Awful worried about it. Kinda peaked lookin'—all shot to pieces, I guess. Can't hardly drag around. Why? Is he somebody you knowed at some time?"

That question was bordering on dangerous ground. The men held their breath, darting a glance at Single-Shot, struck dumb at his daring. Clawsuss' dark face was somber, brooding, and something wild burned for a moment in the agate-green gaze. He remained utterly motionless for a split second, then turned his bison-maned head and slowly looked Single-Shot up and down.

"No, Andy." His eyes veiled the wild light, turned opaque and expressionless under his black brows. "I never knowed him. I just heered of a fella by that name once. But that ain't got nothin' to do with havin' a good time to-night. Come on, Crook, bale 'er out!"

CHAPTER XV
A FLASK OF RAW GOLD

CANYON CENTER roared high until dawn. Clawsuss and Mark were in the middle of things. They ripped the Happy Daze wide open and tried to get everybody drunk. Which wasn't a difficult task, all hands being willing subjects—excepting Crook. No man in Canyon Center had ever seen Crook Alvord drunk.

Mark and Clawsuss tried to accomplish it that night, but finally were forced to give it up as a bad job. They did strive to curb their hilarity enough that the shouts of mirth, their rollicking laughter and barber shop singing would not disturb Garner Blue's family, or the few men living in more or less isolated cabins with their wives. Those men were institutions, also, of a kind. They were in Canyon Center, but not of it. Along toward dawn, satisfied that everybody was happy and that they had made a good job of it, Clawsuss and Mark, cheerfully lit up themselves, took jovial adieu of the stubbornly sober Crook and strolled out of the Happy Daze with Satan between them. They rounded up Ripp and Nigg and started for Buckshot Canyon.

As they passed out of sight of the town and entered a long wooded gulch, Mark looked up at the sky and asked casually, "Ain't you gonna go see him, Clawsuss?"

"I reckon not for a while, yet." Clawsuss' eyes narrowed, and he shook his big head. "I got to have time to sit down, Mark, and kind of think it over, like. I knowed he'd come along someday. But he ain't come the way I been expectin' him to. He's come under his own name—and sick-like, his memory gone. You know how long Butcher Krantz has been hidin'. That means he must have changed his ways somewhat. Of course, I got to see him. But it's gonna take some thinkin' first. When we gits home I'm gonna show yuh how I got that flask of nuggets fixed fer him, and you'll understand."

Mark nodded, but made no reply. It was evening when they finally jogged into Buckshot Canyon and drew up before Hell's Gate. Clawsuss swung out of the saddle and pulled from his pocket the key he used to lock the heavy door of the cabin.

"Yuh go on and put up the hosses, Mark, and I'll go in and git some chuck raked up. When yuh come in I'll show yuh that flask of nuggets."

Mark assented and went on toward the barn with the horses, as Clawsuss ascended the steps, unlocked the door and went into the house. The giant had a roaring fire going in both stoves and deer steak sizzling over the flames when Mark entered. Clawsuss heard the sound of his newly acquired partner's feet in the big living room, and he joined him before the potbellied stove, pointing to a picture on the wall.

It was the marine, in its sharp greens and blues, presenting its wide choppy sea and the clipper ship sailing full-rigged straight into the foreground. The picture had been tacked to a board, and surrounded by a frame which Clawsuss had fashioned of twisted alder twigs. It was the one framed picture on the walls. Mark glanced at it, following Clawsuss' pointing finger, his colorless brows raised in inquiry.

"Just take that pitcher down, Mark, and yuh'll see somethin'," Clawsuss invited, smiling grimly.

Mark walked slowly to the picture and reached to lift it from the nail from which it was suspended. He moved with a conscious feeling of reluctance, sensing something in Clawsuss that made him uneasy. As the picture came down in his fingers he drew a sharp breath and stepped backward.

Behind the picture a box had been sunk into the slab wall. The box was constructed of heavy iron plate, with riveted seams impervious to tampering. Across the front of the box a heavy plate glass gave view into its contents. The glass was criss-crossed and barred with a powerful steel screen. A man might stand and *look* into that box to his heart's content. But he would have the devil's own time gaining access to it. With the picture removed, the opening to the iron box was visible from any angle of the room. Indeed, once a man had a view of the grisly contents of that box he would have hard work keeping fascinated eyes from it.

Squarely in the middle of it sat a half-pint whisky flask, with an old blackened cork jammed into its neck. On top of the cork there were visible several ridges caused by initials cut into it. The flask was half full of big nuggets. Around the flask, facing it, grinning at it hideously, were seven bleached human skulls. Otherwise the iron box was completely empty.

Mark turned to Clawsuss with an involuntary shudder, dragging his fascinated gaze from the grim box. "What you got them skulls in there for?"

"They ain't the real skulls of the men they represent," Clawsuss answered quietly, his voice emotionless, his face hard lined. "They is just some I picked up here and there. As for why they is in there—well, Mark, the Butcher killed seven men for gold, that I knows of. How many others he killed for the same thing or for any other reason, I ain't got no way of knowin'. But of them seven I does know. Them skulls was just to remind him of what he did, when he was in here sittin' around with nothin' to do but think. Leastwise, that's what I put 'em thar for in the first place. But now—"

"Yes, now things is changed," Mark said slowly. "What are you goin' to do?"

"I don't know, Mark," Clawsuss returned, eyeing

Mark with a distressed gaze. "I had it planned how he'd sit around here and stare at them skulls, and at that there flask of nuggets, and think. And he'd think so much he'd go plumb crazy if he didn't git sorry fer what he'd done. I had it figured how he might clean turn over a new leaf. Yuh—yuh kin hang that pitcher back now, Mark."

The giant watched as Mark returned the picture to its nail and hid the grisly iron box. "But now, things *is* kind of changed. I don't know jist what I'm gonna do. Yuh see, I wan't only jist aimin' to make him be punished for what he done, I was wantin' him to git some sense inta his head, too. But I'm kinda stopped now, till I git a look at him and find out more about him. Yuh see?"

"Yeh, I see a damn sight too much to be comfortable," Mark answered grimly. "What say we git the grub going, and talk afterward?"

"Talkin' ain't gonna git you'n me much, Mark." Clawsuss half turned toward the kitchen door. "Single-Shot was tellin' me about Blue's daughter bein' out tuh the diggin's, and I reckon every bit we can learn before *we* go out there ain't gonna hurt us none. Yeah—we're gonna go see Norman all right. But we're gonna go see Jo-Anne Blue first."

CHAPTER XVI
MARK'S DESTINY

BOTH Mark and Clawsuss started for Canyon Center two days later with the feeling of men embarking upon a very precarious sort of mission. Crook had told Clawsuss all he knew of Jo-Anne's reaction to meeting the man Symone. Single-Shot Andy had told him all he knew about the man with the numbed brain, but still Clawsuss knew very little of what he was to find when he came face to face at last with the man who had been Butcher Krantz. It came to his mind that Norman might be playing a game, a very shrewd game, pretending to be hurt and a victim of amnesia, when in reality no such thing had happened. If this should be the case, the giant of Buckshot Canyon believed that he could read through Norman's dissembling. He said as much to Mark, as they rode through the thick forest in the clear cold dawn.

"I don't know about that." Mark frowned, and pursed his lips in a grimace of dubiety. "If a fellow's smart enough to pull a stunt like that in the first place, he ought to be smart enough to fool just about anybody. And from what you say of him, your brother Norman was nobody's fool. It really sounds to me as if he was tellin' the truth about this business of having lost his memory. It's queer he don't remember nothing about himself when he was masquerading as Butcher Krantz, that all his recollection goes back to his childhood. To a big man named George, and a flask full of nuggets. Did it ever strike you as queer that he'd remember you as a big man when he was only a kid at the time you ran away?"

Clawsuss shook his head. "Not at all. I was over six feet tall then and weighed nearly two hundred pounds. Lots of growed up men ain't any bigger than that. And I reckon I musta looked like a mountain to a little shaver like he was. It's the only way he would remember me."

"Yeah, I see." Mark nodded thoughtfully. "But I'm dumber than I thought I was, Clawsuss. All this time I've been worryin' about what would happen if Norman should recognize you when he sees you, and I've been forgettin' that he never saw you grown up and with a beard."

Clawsuss turned deep eyes upon Mark's face. "No," he agreed slowly. "He never did—only when he was Butcher Krantz."

Mark started slightly, and remained silent. That was not an angle which would help matters any. If Symone recognized Clawsuss as the man he once had cheated and tried to kill, thought he had killed, along with the butchered Cass Greggory, such recognition must mean the resurrection of Butcher Krantz. If anything Clawsuss could say, or sight of the flask of nuggets in Clawsuss' possession, could bring alive the entire memory of Norman Symone, that also must mean the resurrection of Butcher Krantz, since Norman Symone and Butcher Krantz had once been one. Had they been separated by that blow on the head, or had they both been annihilated by it, leaving a third man and a stranger in their place?

The issue was terribly involved. Mark made a helpless, deprecating gesture. "It don't look very promising, from any side, does it? I wonder just what a fellow's going to do in a case like that?"

Clawsuss smiled wryly. He had been thinking the same twisted thoughts as Mark. "Reckon I don't know any more than you do, Mark. But this much is shore sartin; yuh could figure it all out a dozen times and when yuh come to it yuh'd jist have to take things as they come and act accordin'. All the figurin' don't do yuh no good. I reckon I ain't gonna do none."

"But," Mark persisted. "Suppose the mere sight of you *does* bring the Butcher back, and he tries to start somethin'?"

"I'm bigger'n he is," Clawsuss said grimly. "And Hell's Gate is waitin' for him."

The two men rode on in silence, thinking, reluctant to give voice to their thoughts. Theirs were very uncomfortable thoughts, and the same thoughts were still with them when they rode into Canyon Center and drew their horses to a halt before Garner Blue's shoe shop.

Inside the shop Blue stood inspecting a heavy piece of tan leather which lay soaking in a pan of water. Deciding that the leather was not yet ready for the last, Blue turned to pick up a shoe that lay waiting a new half sole. As he stepped to fit the shoe over the lasting jack, he heard footsteps at his threshold and raised his eyes to see Clawsuss entering the door, a man who was a stranger to Blue following in Clawsuss' wake. Blue's face lighted. He had a very high regard for the giant of Buckshot Canyon, and though he was curious, as was every other man in Canyon Center, about what strange thing lay hidden in the big man's mystery-shrouded past, he had never allowed that curiosity to cloud his appreciation of the man himself, taken at face value, as men were in the West. He smiled a cordial welcome.

"Well, well, Clawsuss! You haven't been in to see me for a long time. It's certainly good to lay eyes on you again."

Clawsuss returned the greeting in kind. "No, I ain't been in for quite a spell. That's right. I thought it was about time I was droppin' around. I want yuh tuh meet my friend, Mark Alvord. He's come tuh stay with me out at Buckshot Canyon."

Since Jo-Anne had made no mention to Blue of the brother Crook feared, and since neither of them had chanced to see any of the boys since Mark's arrival in Canyon Center, Blue had no knowledge of the twisted currents slowly rising and bearing against the dam the years had built. He only noted that Clawsuss' new friend bore the same name as Crook, and he voiced a very natural remark.

"Pleased to know you, Mark. Pleased to know any friend of Clawsuss. Alvord is the name? You couldn't by any chance be any relation to Crook Alvord?"

Mark nodded emphatically. "You bet! I'm his *only* relative. His brother."

Blue exclaimed his pleasure at meeting a brother to Crook, and said he was certain that Crook had been decidedly remiss in the information he dispensed. "Why, nobody even knew he had a brother. I'll bet he was glad to see you."

There was genuine pleasure on Mark's face as he answered heartily and sincerely; "Yeah, I guess Crook's pretty damn glad I'm come. He was telling us that your daughter sort of wanted to see Clawsuss, and Clawsuss wanted me to meet you, so we thought we'd just get it all over with."

Blue's eyes twinkled. "I had an idea Clawsuss' shoes must be wearing out."

Clawsuss shook his head, but there was no answering smile on his face. "Nope, the shoes ain't wearin' out, Garner. You make 'em too good. Mark's made it sound pretty nice, about our comin' in, and of course it's all true. But you know me, Garner. You know it's kinda my way tuh spit things out without much foolin'. The real truth is that we wanta see Miss Jo-Anne. *I* want tuh see her. I think maybe she knows some things I wanta know."

For a moment Blue made no reply, but stood motionless, gazing steadily into Clawsuss' eyes. He knew instantly and instinctively that it had to do with the strange man Jo-Anne had seen up in Saw Tooth Canyon, the man without a memory who was wandering over the country looking for a big man named George. Was this the key that might unlock the closed door to Clawsuss' shrouded past? If it had nothing to do with him, if he were not the big man named George, why was he here seeking to inquire into what Jo-Anne had learned? Blue's legal mind leaped to a dozen hypotheses, a multitude of queries.

Why come to question Jo-Anne? She had seen very little of the man Symone. Why not wait till Single-Shot Andy or some of The Gang were in town and question them? They had seen more of the man, they knew more many times over than Jo-Anne could know. And Blue realized suddenly the rare astuteness of the giant from Hell's Gate. Clawsuss was a far more clever man than Blue had given him credit for being, and he had never set the big man down for a fool. He divined easily why Clawsuss had come seeking Jo-Anne. Clawsuss quite realized, evidently, the usual unobservance of men, appreciated to the full the value of a woman's intuition: he sought the information to be gained from a woman's habit of deeper analysis over passing things.

Blue's gaze flicked to Mark Alvord. Perhaps Mark too was connected with those long departed days Clawsuss had kept so efficiently hidden. Plainly Mark must at least know of Clawsuss' intent in coming here, of his reason for wanting to see Jo-Anne. Garner Blue had been too long a student of men and man's ways not to feel a little tremor of excitement at the thought of what a drama must be due to unfold before his eyes if he read aright. Clawsuss was too keen not to realize that Jo-Anne had very likely told her father all she had seen and heard in Saw Tooth Canyon, but Blue had more wisdom than one man needed. He nodded assent, his grave eyes on the giant's face.

"Why, surely, Clawsuss. If Jo-Anne knows anything that can be of value or assistance to you in any quarter, she will be only too glad to give you her aid. You and Mark come around to the cabin. She'll be very glad to meet Crook's only brother. She's already half in love with Crook himself. Petey's entirely in love with all the boys. Come along through the gate. We'll just go through the shop this way. It's shorter."

Clawsuss followed Blue through the back room, and Mark followed Clawsuss. They passed a few casual remarks back and forth, and Blue halted them in the shade of the porch of the little dwelling, where the flowering vine had become a mass of dense foliage, with only a scattering pink star-flower remaining here and there. He had caught sight of Jo-Anne and Petey, down the bank of the tree-lined creek, under a tall fragrant balsam poplar. Blue raised his voice in a hail, and Jo-Anne turned, seeing him there with the other two men. He beckoned, and she promptly broke into a swift walk, her face alight with eagerness, her lavender-gray eyes shining like clear amethysts. Petey came trailing behind her, curious and interested as usual. As she drew close, she smiled delightedly, and addressed the huge man beside her father.

"I know! You're Clawsuss. There aren't possibly two men as big as you in one place!"

Clawsuss grinned widely, pleased, captivated by her in an instant. "Yuh're shore right, ma'am. I'm Clawsuss, all right. And this here's my friend, Mark Alvord."

Jo-Anne started violently and her face blanched. Her gaze leaped, searching and probing, to Mark Alvord's face. Mark Alvord! The brother Crook feared because he was so good. The brother Crook had said was bitter inside, because he was so queer and solitary that he could make no friends. She remembered too that Crook had said that that fact hurt Mark, and he had the impulse to hit back. But Clawsuss had called him friend. Her clear and penetrating eyes delved deep into the Mark Alvord Crook had never known.

In one flash of divination she read what only a

woman, perhaps, could have seen. Deep in the lead-gray eyes she plumbed the longing for friendly concourse with his own kind. She saw in the straight proud mouth the high determination that would keep him forever from lowering his standard. She saw enough that she knew Mark Alvord for the kind of man she had despaired of finding in the world that held Victor and Luther. Something had to be done. Something had to be done to inform Mark of Crook's attitude before it was too late. She cut across lots, as only her kind can, and she spoke to the man with the lead-gray eyes as if she had known him all her life.

"But how absurd, for Crook to think that you meant it! You didn't mean it any more than he did, did you?"

And Mark Alvord knew what she meant, knew what Crook must have told her. He shook his head. "No, of course I didn't mean it. We was both simply so mad that we didn't have good sense. But we aren't going to get mad at each other any more. We made it all up, and agreed to be sensible after this."

"Oh, you've seen him!" Jo-Anne caught her breath in quick relief.

"Yes'm." For an instant Mark stared at her in silence. He knew what was happening to him. He was doing what he had sworn he never would do. He was falling in love with a woman, here and now, right on the spot, and he didn't have anything to say about it. He asked impulsively, and never knew how wistful the words sounded; "Was you that scared for him?"

Jo-Anne smiled. "No. For you. After all the fine things Crook said about you, after the way Crook told me how much he'd always loved you, I, like Crook, have been afraid of what you might do to yourself if you came."

Mark stared at her, struck dumb. Crook had told her that he had loved his brother all his life! Words were quite beyond that brother as he stood staring at the girl who was to hold his destiny in her two slender hands. Clawsuss stood gazing from one to the other, reading the whole issue as it took place before his gaze, knowing what every word meant. He looked down at Jo-Anne with intent eyes.

"Yo're kind of direct speakin', ain't yuh, ma'am? I reckon I am, too. We don't have much time for beatin' about the bush out here. We come tuh see if yuh wouldn't tell us what yuh thought of that man yuh met up with in Saw Tooth Canyon. Yuh had a good look at 'im, didn't yuh?"

Jo-Anne nodded, giving back Clawsuss' gaze. "Yes, I did. Just what do you want to know from me?"

"Well, a woman gets things like that sometimes, ma'am, where a man don't. And I was wonderin' if yuh'd judge that the fella's puttin' on, or if he really has lost his memory, the way he pretends."

Jo-Anne answered without hesitation. "There

can't be any doubt about that, Clawsuss. One look into his eyes should be enough for anybody. They're lost, wild, empty. No, the man isn't lying. But he gives one the shivers. And you—are you the big man named George?"

Blue winced at his daughter's temerity. But Clawsuss took no offense. He only smiled, a meager twisted smile that made his whole face sad.

"Yes, ma'am. I guess I am. I'm goin' up tuh see 'im; Single-Shot Andy invited me'n Mark tuh come up and see their diggin's. Somebody told Norman about a big man like me bein' up here, and Norman started this way. But—maybe you know all about it?"

"Yes. Single-Shot told me. He kept Symone there, because he was afraid you *might* be the big man named George, and he didn't want any trouble arising for you." Jo-Anne frowned, vastly troubled. She knew instinctively that Clawsuss would tell no more, now. He had only admitted his identity because he had realized that she would know it anyway. She felt the currents of wild, fierce passions rising, beating against the dam years had builded. Something told her that a storm was going to thunder about her head, that before the mystery was unveiled the dam would fall, the torrents would be loosed, hearts would break and men would die. She shivered, as if a cold wind had blown upon her. Her eyes swerved to Mark Alvord.

"Is there anything I can do?" Although she knew as she said it that there was nothing anyone could do.

Clawsuss stood silent, and Mark was dumb. No one knew what to say. And they all started like people prodded by needles, whirling to look, at Petey's shout of delirious joy.

"Oh, Mother! Ain't he grand! Gee, that's a real honest-to-God man-size dawg!"

Jo-Anne repressed a frightened cry. Mark Alvord went white, and Clawsuss took one step forward. Blue stood like a stone.

Just emerged from the back room of the shop, stalking majestically toward them across the garden, came the Great Dane Mark had trained to kill. Petey was running straight toward him, both little arms outstretched, his yellow hair glistening in the sun, his small face beatific. Jo-Anne knew from the attitude of the men that the big dog was dangerous, but she knew also that they had all seen the child's reckless action too late. Even as Clawsuss took that one leap forward, the child reached the dog. He tried to throw his arms around the massive neck, but he couldn't reach it.

Satan halted short and bowed his kingly head. His long tail wagged. He thrust out his red tongue and licked the enraptured child on the cheek. Clawsuss gasped, and raised one hand to wipe away the sweat that had started on his upper lip and forehead.

"By Gawd," the giant breathed. "That's one time I was scared stiff."

Mark's voice came from beyond Clawsuss, cold, level, weighted. "I reckon not—it wouldn't have happened, I mean. I was quicker than him once. I could be again."

Every eye turned upon him. He was still standing motionless, just as he had been, but in his right hand a leveled gun covered Satan. It continued to cover the big dog as Petey turned about and marched toward them, the mighty animal towering above his head.

"I left him out at the hitchin' rack with the hosses," Clawsuss explained. "I reckon he got tired of waitin' and trailed us in here."

"Oh, *your* dog, Clawsuss?" Blue asked in surprise. "I didn't know you had a dog."

"I ain't had him very long. Mark give him to me." And Clawsuss went on to expatiate upon the merits of Satan, his wisdom and his dependability.

He made Satan acquainted with Jo-Anne, with as much ceremony as if the dog had been a human being. The talk continued to revolve about the Great Dane till Clawsuss said it was time for them to take their leave. So, skillfully, the giant evaded reopening the topic of his errant brother and went across the garden walk with Satan in his wake. Petey, standing close to Jo-Anne, for once was silent, staring after the great dog in speechless admiration. Only then did Mark Alvord return his gun to its holster. As he started to turn away, his right hand still resting on the butt of the cedar-handled weapon, he turned his gray eyes upon Jo-Anne.

"Don't think Clawsuss is careless of his manners, Miss Jo-Anne. We both thank you for the information about Norman, but Clawsuss didn't want to bring up the subject again."

"No explanations necessary, Mark." Jo-Anne smiled warmly. "I quite understand. I'm very glad you came, both of you. But I'm especially glad to have met *you,* to know you're here and have everything all straightened out with Crook. Anytime you're in town and have the leisure, I'd be very glad to have you come and see me again."

Something glowed in Mark's lonely hungry eyes, and something brightened his gaunt face. "Yes ma'am. You bet! I was going to ask you if I could come." And he turned to follow Clawsuss across the garden and out of the shop.

"Whew! What a dog!" ejaculated Blue. "He had my hair standing on end there for a minute. Petey, I fear you're a reckless little devil." He glanced down at the child with a reproving shake of the head. Then his gaze lifted to Jo-Anne's face. "What a strange man this Mark Alvord is!"

"Yes," Jo-Anne agreed. And she thought of the gun leveled upon the dog, so swiftly, to guard Petey from harm. Any man who could move that quickly must have spent years acquiring such facility. Slower than Crook? He might have been once. And she divined suddenly something of the answer to it, to his meeting with Crook. He had come seeking Crook, after he had made himself proficient with the weapon of which Crook was master. He had come seeking him, and, having become the quicker of the two, he had commanded the situation and made his peace with the brother who feared him because he was so good. "Yes," the girl repeated. "Strange—but what a man."

Blue was conscious of a little quiver of alarm. Did Jo-Anne admire this man with the deft gun-hands, with the cruel strength in his bleak gray eyes? "He's a killer," Blue said grimly, his gaze following Petey, who had gone trotting up the bank to paddle in the creek.

"Of course," Jo-Anne assented, undisturbed. "But I've learned one thing, Dad. There's no halfway business in this world. It's kill or be killed. And somehow I don't believe I'd want me or mine to belong to the 'be killed' class. Yes—he's a killer." And in her mind's eye she saw him crowded by danger, hewing his way coolly and relentlessly, undaunted and undismayed. She added softly, "Maybe, sometime, we might have reason to be glad that he is."

"Whatever makes you say a thing like that?" demanded Blue quickly.

Jo-Anne's amethyst eyes returned his probing

gaze. "I don't know. I just have what the boys call a hunch. There's something terrible brewing, and it has to do with Clawsuss and that man up in Saw Tooth Canyon, that Norman Symone."

CHAPTER XVII

"SOMEBODY NAMED GEORGE"

It was well into the afternoon of the next day when Clawsuss and Mark Alvord arrived at the diggings where Single-Shot Andy and The Gang were busily at work wresting the gold from the alluvial soil that had been washed there so long ago. Yellowjacket Bevans came walking out to meet them, with a jovial greeting, informing them that Single-Shot was up at the dam but would be down presently. He invited Clawsuss and Mark to get down and stretch their legs and have a look around.

Horse-Pistol Mike took upon himself the rôle of guide, while Yellowjacket went back to aid Shy Bolcom in taking up the rifles, and proudly escorted Clawsuss and Mark all over the canyon, completing his tour of inspection at the dam. There they met Single-Shot, who was just about to return to the camp. Single-Shot greeted his guests with delight and enthusiasm.

"Yuh seen all the diggin's?" he asked. "But I guess you have all right, with Mike doin' the honors. He wouldn't let yuh miss nothin'. How yuh like the place?"

"Shore looks like a regular bonanzy," Clawsuss approved, heartily. "About the best lookin' layout I've seen in I don't know when."

The men walked back to the camp together, discussing the merits of the mine and the possible extent of its workings. It was not until after the evening meal, when Clawsuss, Mark and Andy were sitting to one side, that Clawsuss brought into the conversation mention of the thing that had brought him there.

"What about this fella Symone, Andy?" Clawsuss queried casually. "Has he gone away? We didn't see nothin' of him as we come up."

Single-Shot Andy answered him in quite as casual a tone. "No. He ain't gone nowhere, Clawsuss. He probably was in his cabin. You can't see it from the trail. We kin go over tuhmorra and have a talk with him, if yuh'd like. He's a real interestin' fella."

Single-Shot Andy maintained that air of casualness and neutrality, but he was a very alert and prepared man when, riding at Clawsuss' side and a little ahead of Mark, they arrived within sight of Norman Symone's small prospecting layout the next morning. Again, Norman was nowhere in sight, so Andy led the way to his hidden cabin. He rapped on the door, as Clawsuss and Mark swung from their horses and advanced to stand at his shoulder. Clawsuss stood utterly motionless, as the door swung wide and Norman Symone stood before them.

As Single-Shot started to speak, to make some explanation of their presence there, the voice of Clawsuss spoke sharply in his ear.

"Keep still. Let him alone, and see if he recognizes anybody."

The man in the doorway frowned. And though he was changed, so changed that a less concerned eye might have failed to identify him, Clawsuss knew him instantly for the man he pretended to be. There could be no doubt of it, it was the man who had killed Cass Greggory, the man who had terrorized the frontier under the alias of Butcher Krantz, who confronted the giant from Hell's Gate.

All resemblance to the Butcher was so neutralized as to have become insignificant. The once heavy body had shrunk to such a state of emaciation that its very lines were changed. The oddly ape-like face was so gaunt and drained of color that the scar on the left cheek, faded to a thin white line, was almost invisible. The dark brown hair that the Butcher had worn in a stiff bristle presented an entirely different appearance in that long sweep of shining waves. Even the little white patch of hair on the left temple added to the complete change wrought in his looks. But the change in the expression of his face was the most conspicuous thing evident to Clawsuss' searching eyes.

The brutal, glowering, threatening expression that had grown habitual with Butcher Krantz had given way to an air of bewilderment, had been superseded by a strange wildness in the eyes, and under all and above all the man was literally permeated by an unpleasant air of sly cunning.

He greeted Single-Shot with a bare nod, and his gaze went on to Clawsuss. His eyes widened, something in them seemed to grow still, as if he were listening for something, and his lips moved, but he made no sound. He glanced at Mark, then his gaze came back to fasten on Clawsuss.

"Are you the big fellow I came up here to see?" he asked suddenly.

"I guess I am," Clawsuss replied.

"Well, you're big enough, surely," Symone muttered. "But you don't look like anybody I ever saw before. Is your name George?"

"My name is Clawsuss," said the man from Hell's Gate. "Won't nobody do but a man named George?"

"No," returned Symone sharply. "I've been looking for him too long even to think of giving up now—or ever. I have to find him. I'm getting tired of not knowing who I am."

"But you do know who you are," Mark put in. "What's a name, anyway?"

"Yes, that's just it!" Symone retorted with surprising and unexpected vehemence. "I know my name—but what good does that do? I don't know where I've ever been, or whom I've seen or what I've done. Those are the things I want to know. If I ever find George, he can tell me. He was an awfully big man, as I have him in mind, what mind I've got. But he wasn't so big as you." His gaze challenged Clawsuss. "Do *you* know any big man named George?"

"I've known a lot of Georges," the giant told him evenly. "You better come on over tuh my place and rest and lay around fer a spell. Me'n Mark, here, 'd like tuh have yuh real well."

"But I haven't time to go visiting anybody," Symone replied, looking at Clawsuss in astonishment. "Now I've learned that you're not the man I'm looking for, I'll have to be getting on."

Clawsuss glanced at Mark. He couldn't *let* Norman go on. He knew it, and Mark knew it. They must get him to Hell's Gate, if they had to take him there by force. Clawsuss spoke with the air of a man striving to be sociable and entertaining.

"I shore wisht yuh'd change yore mind. We don't see many strangers out here, and we always like tuh have a chance tuh visit with 'em and show 'em a good time before they goes on. They's lots of curious things around here to see. Why, fer instance, I know a man that's got a whisky flask with a lotta nuggets in it, and he won't take 'em out and buy nothin' with 'em because they're a kind of keepsake of somebody he knowed once."

Clawsuss' speech stopped short, for the effect of his words on the man in the doorway was instantaneous and startling. The wild eyes blazed, for a moment clarified by the light of perfect sanity. The white face flushed with color. The slack jaw set and squared. But only for an instant. It was gone as quickly as it had come, to be succeeded by an air of bewilderment even greater than before.

"A flask of nuggets," he said slowly. "Why, that's something else I'm looking for. I guess you didn't know it. If I came to your house to stay a while, could I get to see that man?"

Clawsuss nodded. "Yes. Yuh'd get tuh see him all right. I'll promise yuh that."

"Then I'll come," said Symone promptly. "When shall we go?"

Mark and Single-Shot Andy looked on in silence as Clawsuss made his maneuver, won his point, and completed arrangements to return to Hell's Gate with Norman Symone as his guest. The three miners returned to the diggings, where Clawsuss and Mark would bid The Gang good-by and prepare for the return trip. Speech was a flat thing between the three, banal, barren, meaningless; the speech of men cautiously skirting the edge of a mysterious and tacitly forbidden subject, none daring to bring it into the open. When Clawsuss and Mark rode away from the diggings, a few hours later, Single-Shot Andy stood staring after them, turning over in his mind the things he had learned. They were not things to be passed on to another, nor were they things that rendered him any too comfortable in the possession of them.

Clawsuss still remained to him the mystery man of Hell's Gate. But he knew two things about Clawsuss now that he had not known before. He knew that Clawsuss had in his possession a whisky flask containing nuggets. And he knew that Clawsuss was somebody named George.

When, a couple of hours later, Horse-Pistol Mike asked him what had become of Norman Symone (Mike had ridden by the cabin and had seen the evidence of Norman's departure) Single-Shot told him bluntly that Norman had gone away with Clawsuss and Mark. Mike informed the rest of The Gang, and no one said anything beyond that. No one asked any questions. Asking questions wasn't according to the code of the West, but a man may always think. And every man in The Gang knew what Andy had known, knew that Clawsuss was somebody named George; and they felt with alarming certitude that the whole town of Canyon Center was henceforth going to be sitting on a powder magazine—waiting for somebody to drop a match.

CHAPTER XVIII
FLOOD WATERS

BEFORE a dam breaks, there is sometimes a reflex in the gathering forces; as if the straining waters draw back within themselves to gain power for the final surge, when the devastating crown sweeps everything before it, crushing and battering, leaving wreckage and desolation in its wake. So the forces gathering to flood Canyon Center drew within themselves. For a disarming little while nothing of any moment or portent happened.

Norman Symone wandered about Hell's Gate like a lost man, remembering nothing, restless, with childish insistence asking Clawsuss to produce the man who had the whisky flask full of nuggets. Clawsuss put him off patiently and skillfully, observing him covertly and searching for some point of contact in the dulled brain that could be used as a touchstone without wreaking utter disaster. Mark Alvord looked on in vague uneasiness, and held his tongue, knowing that the one reason the giant had for withholding the flask that might bring the errant mind back was sheer fear of the consequences. Norman fretted, and Mark's uneasiness increased, but Clawsuss was obdurate. Mark went into Canyon Center twice to see Jo-

Anne and Petey, and took Satan along for Petey's delight. To the unvoiced curiosity of both Blue and Jo-Anne he explained that Clawsuss had brought Norman to stay at Hell's Gate for a while, but Norman remembered nothing and would doubtlessly go his way very soon. He told no more than that, and succeeded in giving them the impression that, after all, the issue between Clawsuss and the man Symone was of no importance and unworthy even of their interest. He turned the conversation to things mutually interesting to himself and Jo-Anne, and they grew to know more of each other, to see more surely that their ideas and ideals were compatible, their paths bent in the same direction.

Mark returned from a visit to Jo-Anne to find Clawsuss alarmed and upset. Norman had disappeared, had taken his horse and all his small effects with him, and Clawsuss had no least clew as to which way he had gone. And Canyon Center gasped, and looked to its defense, and shuddered to know that the thing it had feared so long had transpired at last.

Butcher Krantz had kept his vow and was come.

Garner Blue was the first man to hear of it, and Crook Alvord was the first man to know it. Crook took himself in hand after the first shock of realization and called at Blue's shop shortly after daybreak.

Jo-Anne and Petey were only just up, and Petey was showing Blue the little rock cave he had builded on the creek bank while Jo-Anne was beginning preparations for breakfast.

Crook came hurrying in the little side gate that gave onto the side road, and in his impatient gait there was some unusual sound that caused Blue to turn and look. Then he saw Crook's face, hastily left Petey to his play and came striding swiftly toward Crook, startled and dismayed. The face he had always seen florid and good humored was quite colorless, drawn about the mouth. The strained look in Crook's eyes, the whole air of the man, told Blue that something shocking had occurred.

"For God's sake what has happened, Crook?" he asked sharply, and Jo-Anne, within the cabin, heard the startled tone, the alarming words, and came running out the open door to halt and stare at Crook's haggard face.

Crook looked from one to the other. He could find no easy words. "Butcher Krantz has showed up," he said hoarsely. "There's no tellin' what's going to happen. This town's going to be no place for you and Petey, Jo-Anne. You, Garner—you get her away from here before it's too late. Get her away and keep her away till somebody cuts that devil down at the roots. Get her away! Butcher Krantz has come, and there's goin' to be hell popping!"

138

Blue lost color a little, and turned startled eyes on his daughter. "I suspect I should," he admitted. "If what I've heard of Butcher Krantz is true. Are you positive, Crook? Who was telling you? You're certain there's no mistake?"

"Mistake?" Crook laughed gratingly. "I wish to God there was. But there ain't. Nobody was tellin' me. I seen him with my own eyes—and I know him. I tell you you got to get Jo-Anne out of here!"

"I agree with you," Blue replied without hesitation. "But you've come upon me unawares with your ugly news, Crook. I can't gather my wits to think where I shall take her."

"There's only one place *to* take her!" Crook turned to Jo-Anne with entreaty on every line of his drawn face. "Get ready quick, Jo-Anne. You and your dad take Petey and go out to Hell's Gate with Clawsuss and Mark. That house of Clawsuss' is like a fort. Nobody will get in to bother you in that cabin! But send Mark to me. Tell him I want him, quick. Don't say nothin' to anybody else, and tell Mark to keep it dark. I'm layin' a trap for the Butcher, and if the whole town finds out he's showed up it'll knock my plans intuh a cocked hat."

"But Crook!" Jo-Anne eyed him steadily, penetratingly. "You told me once you weren't afraid of Butcher Krantz. You—"

"I'm afraid now," Crook interrupted harshly. "Afraid for you and Petey. You folks all get out there to Hell's Gate as quick as you can saddle Garner's horses and ride. Don't even stop for breakfast—take something along and eat your grub on the way. Get there! That's the one thing you got to think about. And when you get there, send Mark foggin' it in to me as fast as he can come."

Both Blue and Jo-Anne gave him an unqualified promise to do as he asked. Neither had any slightest idea of refusing. They knew well enough that if Crook begged them to go so urgently his reasons were cogent and well founded. There could be no question of hesitation.

Crook returned to the Happy Daze, after helping Blue saddle the horses, but before Crook ever reached the saloon Blue and his daughter and adopted grandson were well on the way to Hell's Gate.

It was evening when they descended into Buckshot Canyon, and approached the big cabin Clawsuss had built. Mark had seen them coming, and emerged from the house smiling a delighted welcome, exclaiming over the unexpected guests. He did not notice how sober were those guests till he reached up to take the sleeping Petey from Blue's arms. Then he caught the expression on the shoemaker's face.

"What's the matter?" he asked quickly. "Has anything happened?"

"I fear so," Blue replied, swinging out of the

saddle and standing facing Mark. "I fear, though, that something else may happen, some unguessed but very terrible thing. Crook feared it first. That's why we're here."

Behind Mark, Clawsuss appeared in the doorway, half hidden by the thick vine climbing over the porch. He saw the tense tableau there in the yard but a few feet away, the features of all of them clear to him in the rays of the setting summer sun. Jo-Anne had also dismounted and had drawn close to her father. They both stood facing Mark, and Mark had about him a startled listening air, as he held the sleeping boy close, waiting to hear what Blue had to tell. To Clawsuss the whole group had an alarming air of portent, and he halted involuntarily, listening to catch every word. He heard Mark say:

"You mean to tell me Crook's afraid of anything on earth?"

"He was afraid for Jo-Anne," Blue said steadily. "Butcher Krantz has put in an appearance. Crook asked me to bring Jo-Anne and Petey and come out here to stay, where she and the child would be out of all harm's way, till Krantz is apprehended and put where he belongs."

Clawsuss spoke, and his voice was harsh and tense. "How does Crook know?"

For the first time Blue became aware of the giant's presence. For the first time since their arrival Jo-Anne spoke.

"Crook saw him, Clawsuss." The girl was color-less and weary, but her amethyst eyes were steady with the courage that never flagged. "The Butcher looked through the window into the Happy Daze, and Crook knows him. He says there's no telling what might happen. So he sent us out here. But he wants you, Mark. He wants you to come in as quickly as you can."

Again Clawsuss spoke from the doorway, and started across the porch toward them. "Well, come on in, folks. Come on in and have a bite to eat, and do a little restin' up. Give me the boy, Mark. You go on and put the hosses up. Come on in, Garner, you'n Jo-Anne must be awful tired."

Mark glanced from the shoemaker to his daughter with a little startled and half shamefaced grimace. "You'll have to excuse me. I was so sur-prised and upset that I was forgetting all about my manners. You go on in the house with Clawsuss. I'll be right in soon as I get the horses put up."

Clawsuss took the sleeping child and turned to go back into the house, and only Mark knew what a colossal effort the giant must have made to retain his self-control when he heard the grim news Blue had brought. So the Butcher had come to life! Mark revolved the thought in his head as he glanced up at Blue and Jo-Anne ascending the steps to the house, and he started toward the barn with the horses. He knew as no one else could know, save the giant himself, what that news would mean to Clawsuss. It would mean that all hope was gone of retrieving Norman from the doom Butcher Krantz had shaped for himself.

All the way to the barn and back, while he was putting up the horses, while he was tossing them down their portion of wild hay, measuring out their oats, while he was returning slowly to the cabin with feet that dragged, he was trying to find something to say to Clawsuss when they two should be alone, and knew that there was nothing he could say.

He entered the living room to find Blue standing in the doorway that gave onto the kitchen, and Jo-Anne in the kitchen helping Clawsuss get together a hot supper. All three of them were talking, with forced cheerfulness, of casual subjects, and Mark knew instinctively that Clawsuss had closed the subject of Butcher Krantz, and would not reopen it again till it became imperative. Jo-Anne glanced up at Mark as he entered the kitchen.

"This place is just as lovely as you said it was, Mark. And I certainly agree with you that it took a lot of ingenuity to erect such a building. But Clawsuss, what odd names you use out here. And why do you have bars over the windows—like a jail?"

Clawsuss' answer was the essence of nonchalance. "Well, ma'am, when I first came out here they was a lot of dangerous animals about, cougars, panthers, yuh know, and such. I didn't want 'em comin' in and makin' a meal off me when I was sleepin' peaceful, so I just kind of fixed it up to keep 'em out. Yuh wanta remember I'm pretty much off to myself, here in Buckshot Canyon."

"Well, you certainly took plenty of precaution," Jo-Anne commented, with a little uneasy laugh. She turned to Mark with a worried question. "When are you going in to see what Crook wants, Mark?"

"To-night," Mark replied promptly. "If Crook said for me to come right away, that's what he meant for me to do. I'll probably get an hour or two of sleep and strike out about midnight. You better watch that coffee pot, Jo-Anne. It boils over awful easy."

As if one coffee pot could boil over any easier than another. But Jo-Anne saw that for some unknown reason both Clawsuss and Mark wanted to avoid discussion of the subject of Butcher Krantz and his advent into Canyon Center. She let the subject lie, and none of them mentioned it again till it came bedtime and Clawsuss showed them to their rooms.

Clawsuss took Mark in to sleep with him, and put Blue up in the room Mark had occupied. Both of these chambers were downstairs. Upstairs there was but the large, roomy attic. Here Clawsuss quartered Jo-Anne and Petey.

"And I'm gonna leave Satan here on guard at your door," Clawsuss informed the girl. "No harm could come to yuh with that boy on the watch. I'll be sayin' good night, now, ma'am. I suspect Mark will want tuh be gittin' off, and I want tuh have a talk with him before he goes. Good night, ma'am. Sleep easy. Yo're safe."

"Yes." The girl smiled after the giant stepped inside her doorway and glanced down at the Great Dane lying obediently in front of the door where Clawsuss had bade him stay. The girl called softly after Clawsuss' disappearing back: "Good night, Clawsuss. And—thank you."

Down in the living room Mark was waiting alone, pacing impatiently back and forth, as Clawsuss came in. Mark halted, and Clawsuss stopped, and for a moment the two men stood surveying each other in a pregnant silence. Then Clawsuss said, "Well, I guess that settles it."

Mark frowned, his face pale with distress. "I wish there might be some mistake, but I reckon there isn't."

"No, there ain't no mistake." Clawsuss dropped down into a chair, his face gray with resignation. "All my hopin' and plannin', all my waitin', fer nothin'. No, we can't be idiots enough tuh try tuh believe that Crook was mistaken. Unless—unless Crook saw Norman, and knew him for who he was in spite of the changes, and got scared all fer nothin'. I didn't know Crook had ever seen the Butcher at all. And Crook may have just seen him lookin' through the window that way, and not have knowed that he was the same fella Andy had been talkin' about that had lost his memory. That way, he wouldn't know that the Butcher was as good as dead and there wasn't no harm in him."

"I've been thinking of that." Mark sighed and frowned. "I hope that's the way it is. I'll beat it right in there to see Crook and get the lay of things. If that's the way of it, I'll explain to Crook and tell him not to say anything and go getting the whole town stirred up all for nothing. The more I think of it, the more I'm inclined to believe that's what's happened. About the size of it, Clawsuss, Norman got tired waitin' for you to produce them nuggets, and started out on a still hunt for himself, was just snoopin' around to see what he could see and looked in the window. And Crook recognized him and got scared."

"Did *you* know Crook had ever met up with the Butcher?"

Mark shook his head in negation. "No, I didn't, Clawsuss. He never even so much as mentioned him to me. But then, you want to remember I ain't seen any too much of Crook in the last few years. And I guess sittin' around here and talkin' isn't going to do either of us any good. We'd better turn in. I'll get enough sleep to take the edge off, then I'll get up and hit for Canyon Center. And don't let her worry." Mark gestured upward significantly. "Until we know there's something to worry about."

CHAPTER XIX
THE FORBIDDEN ROOM

THE next morning Jo-Anne insisted on helping Clawsuss get breakfast, and Petey romped around the yard with Satan till Blue called him in to eat. After breakfast Petey went out again with the dog, and Jo-Anne told Clawsuss that she was going to take charge of the kitchen.

"I think I'll just take charge of the whole house from now on," she announced to the owner of Hell's Gate. "When we're gone again you can come back to cooking flapjacks and washing dishes all you please. But I've got to have something to do. I'm not one of these people who can sit around placidly with folded hands. So I'm going to clean up this house and make a regular job of it. Why look at the cobwebs all over—and the dust!"

"No'm—I don't want yuh should go tearin' down the dust and cobwebs in this here room!" Clawsuss interposed hastily, his eyes flashing, veiled, to the picture hanging over the iron box. "If yuh please, ma'am," he went on earnestly, turning his gaze to her surprised face, "yuh kin dust and clean the other rooms all yuh want. But this is the room where I allers sit, and I've got kind of used to them cobwebs. It wouldn't seem like home if they was tore down."

147

Jo-Anne wrinkled her brows in a frown of mock reproof. "All right, if you command, you hopeless bachelor. I'll have to leave your precious old cobweb festoons untouched here. But as for that beautiful big attic room you turned over to Petey and me, and the kitchen, I'm going to have them all spic and span. I will admit that this room is picturesque the way it is now, cobwebs and all. It might be admitted a shame to spoil it. But surely you won't object if I sweep the floor?"

"No'm, I reckon not. I sweep it myself, once in a while." Clawsuss grinned, and his gaze moved casually to the opposite wall, where the marine scene was looped with cobwebs draping from the slab walls. Mark's act of removing the picture to look into the box a while past had disturbed the gauzelike webs a little, but they had re-formed themselves into unbroken gray festoons in the intervening time. The giant nodded agreeably. "Yuh can jist go ahead and make yoreself to home, ma'am, so long as yuh don't monkey with this room here. How'd yuh like the look of Buckshot Canyon, Jo-Anne?"

"It looks good to me!" Jo-Anne plied her broom vigorously. "I'm beginning to feel like a new man already. Last night I had to force myself to eat your excellent dinner, but this morning I was hungry as a bear. I wish you'd show me how to use a pick and pan, Clawsuss. I'd like to wash some real gold out of the dirt with my own hands. And if I got it, I'd consider it worth panning all the dirt in Buckshot Canyon."

"Well, rest yoreself and wait till I git my beans hoed and I'll be glad to show yuh. Satan—whar you been?" Clawsuss turned to the Great Dane as the animal stalked in the door following Petey and Blue, and flopped down at his feet.

"Why, he followed us," Blue explained, his eyes on the dog's huge head. "Petey and I went for a walk up the canyon. Satan had to go too. He's friendly, in spite of his formidable appearance, isn't he?"

"I wouldn't say he's friendly," Clawsuss answered. "He's just took to you folks. He's really pretty mean—reg'lar killer, raised thataway. Jo-Anne and Petey ain't afraid of him and he knows it. Reckon if he knowed anybody was afraid of him he'd run 'em plumb to death."

"A killer! Is he?" Jo-Anne paused in the kitchen doorway, a flour-sack dishrag in her hand, and gazed intently at the big dog. "I don't doubt you, Clawsuss. But he and I get on all right. Come here, Satan. I'll give you some dinner. Come on!" The Great Dane rose and stalked majestically into the kitchen and Petey followed him.

Blue pursed his lips and looked after the dog. "Yes, I guess he could be pretty mean, if he were aroused. I'd hate to have him take after me. I'd hate to have that dog take after anyone I didn't want to see killed."

At work in the adjoining room, Jo-Anne caught some of their words and her uneasy thoughts were aroused again. She had been striving valiantly to retain the casual air she wore outwardly. But in spite of herself her thoughts would mull ceaselessly about this mystery-haunted cabin to which she had been banished for her own safety. She wondered why Clawsuss kept that huge dog, and why the dog had been trained to kill. She wondered why Clawsuss did not want her to dust the big living room. What was there in that room that he did not want moved? What was there he did not want her to see? Why those bars on the windows, and the lame excuse he had given for their presence? Why that massive lock on the door? And why call such a beautiful place Hell's Gate?

Covertly she scrutinized Clawsuss' dark expressionless face numerous times that morning, and wondered what went on behind the mask.

Plenty was going on behind that impenetrable front. Behind that stoical exterior Clawsuss was a man on the rack. He had come to feel a powerful yearning toward the man who was his brother and did not know him at all. Yet the grim memory of the murdered Cass, and of the stolen money that beloved partner had worked so hard to save, did not lessen its grip. Nor did the memory fade of the leering laugh with which Butcher Krantz strode out the door after venting his fury on two men, leaving them bloody and still, thinking he was leaving two dead instead of one. The old implacable desire for vengeance in Cass's name rose furiously when Clawsuss recalled the things Butcher Krantz had done.

Yet, he argued with himself, was it just to hold to account for the Butcher's brutalities that queerly pitiful, suspiciously antagonistic and bewildered being who was the Norman Symone of to-day? Clawsuss was not at all self-deceived as to why he had continually put Norman off, refusing to let him know who had the nuggets and where they were, nor was he in the least ashamed, even in his own eyes, of his enervating fear of the consequences were even the smallest part of the dull brain brought alive. He was most concerned now to know whether or not he and Mark had guessed right, whether or not the man Crook had seen through the window was really Norman Symone as he was or the fiendish killer come to life. And because of his harassed thoughts he was doubly grateful for the presence of the shoemaker and his little family, grateful for anything to occupy his attention till Mark should return.

CHAPTER XX
BUTCHER KRANTZ

MARK, meanwhile, was nearing Canyon Center. He rode steadily, but not hurriedly, since he was fairly certain in his own mind that Crook had merely seen Norman engaged on his still hunt for the flask of nuggets, and Crook would have no way of knowing that the Butcher had become a harmless halfwit.

It was after noon when Mark reached Happy Daze, early afternoon, and the saloon was not so deserted as it usually was at that hour. Several men were grouped around the bar, talking desultorily about nothing in particular. Crook sighed in relief as Mark came through the swing doors, and poured out a foam-topped glass of beer to quench Mark's thirst. Mark took a deep draught of the cool beer, then leaned on the bar and addressed Crook in an undertone.

"What's all this about the Butcher showing up, Crook?"

"Wait till you've drunk your beer," Crook replied, glancing at the men lined along the bar. "Then we'll go in the little private back room and talk. I don't want to do no chinnin' where these galoots can hear."

"I can drink beer any time." Mark started to shove his glass back from him. "Let's git—"

"No, no! Go ahead and bale it into yuh." Crook raised a protesting hand. "You might feel like you want something stronger before we get done talkin'."

Mark made short work of the beer, and motioned for Crook to lead the way. He followed down the room as Crook went down the bar, and found at the end of the bar a door that opened into the private room in the rear.

It was a small room, Mark noticed, as he entered it in Crook's wake. It contained little save a small table, three chairs and some odds and ends. A large coal oil lamp was on the table, by a ragged deck of cards and an old cracked dish with a handful of pretzels in it. Several empty bottles were scattered about the room. Two calendars were on the wall; one bearing the picture of a glorified honky-tonk Mamie in very bright pink tights, and one depicting a forest fire more lurid than any forest fire ever was. Both calendars were years old. A sturdy little black clock with a tuneful spring-gong inside sat on a rough board shelf where it could be seen by any one sitting at the table.

A door led from the room to the outside, diagonally across the room from the door opening into the saloon. Only one window was in the room, a rather large window. Years before one of the girls in the Blazin' Sin had given Pete Cobalt an old gauzy skirt of hers, telling him mockingly it was a keepsake to remember her by when she was gone.

Pete had ripped a piece of the cotton net from the full-gathered goods and hung it over the window in the back room for a curtain. It was still there.

Crook closed the door leading into the saloon, and gestured Mark to a chair. Mark seated himself by the table, and glanced curiously out of the window, the window through which Crook had seen the Butcher peering. Mark saw nothing but the branches of trees and a patch of sky. There was nothing behind the saloon but a rubbish heap and a trail leading off through the forest.

"What was he doing outside the window?" Mark asked, as Crook dropped into the chair across the table, facing him.

"Not a damn thing, Mark." Crook shrugged. "Just stood there, lookin' over the room, till he got a look at me. I'd started into the saloon, but I heard him kick over a can and I turned to look—you can see right through that stuff Pete put up for a curtain, night or day. I could see his face as plain as anything, the lamp here gives a damn strong light, and it lit him up good."

"I reckon you got het up all for nothin', though, Crook." Mark doggedly adhered to the casual tone he had maintained since he first entered the saloon. "You know that fella Jo-Anne was telling you about? The one that's been prospectin' just below their diggin's in Saw Tooth Canyon?"

"Sure." Crook stared slightly. "What the hell's he got to do with it?"

"More'n you'd think, Crook. I got to tell you some of another man's business, and that's a thing I don't never do. But I've *got* to do it now so you'll understand. This Norman Symone is Clawsuss' brother, Crook."

"The hell!" Crook stared; his stare became wide and unbelieving. He shook his head as if he couldn't quite comprehend what Mark had said. "Clawsuss' *brother!* You can't mean it."

"Reckon Clawsuss could have a brother as well as you." Mark smiled dryly. "But the point is, Crook, that Clawsuss' brother—used to be the Butcher." And he went on, swiftly, as concisely as possible, to tell Crook the story of George Symone, Norman Symone, Cass Greggory and the Butcher, of Clawsuss in his cabin at Hell's Gate waiting for the Butcher to show up from somewhere. "So you see how it is, Crook," Mark concluded. "When he did come, here he is only about half there on account of somebody hitting him over the head with a rock, and all he remembers is a big fella named George and that flask of nuggets. What he was doin' around looking in windows ain't so mysterious when you come to think about it. He's on a still hunt for the fella that has them nuggets, and if he'd see somebody in a little back room like this all by themselves, it's certain he'd take a good look to make sure whether or not the man in the room was countin' his nuggets or some fool thing like that. Never can tell what a person with a damaged brain might think about things. What's the matter, Crook?"

Crook sat staring at him, both hands gripped on the edge of the table, his florid face gone pasty, all expression wiped from it.

"Come out of it, man!" Mark thrust out a hand, gripped Crook's arm and shook it. "What ails you, anyway? Are you that scared of what's left of Butcher Krantz? I wish to hell that the fella who socked him with a rock had made a good job of it."

"It wasn't a rock," said Crook stiffly. "It was a gun barrel."

Mark's hand went still on his brother's arm. "How the hell do you know?"

"Because it was me that crocked him one," said Crook harshly, and suddenly his pasty face was alive with emotion and excitement. "Him and me run up against each other right after you'n me split. He tried to get at me with that damn knife of his, but he'd struck one man too quick for him. I shot him down, then I cracked his head in with my gun barrel to make good and sure he was dead. How he ever lived after what I done to him is more'n I can understand."

"But why didn't you ever guess it was him up there in Saw Tooth Canyon? A fella from Californy, that had been hit over the head and lost his memory. Seems like you'd a guessed he might be the Butcher."

"How would I?" demanded Crook, rather hotly.

156

"I was so damn sure I'd killed him. Why, I shot him first, I tell you! And I knowed what he was, what he'd done to so many people. Not men alone, either. He was hell for the women. That's why I sent Jo-Anne out to Hell's Gate hot-foot. Think of what he done to Cass Greggory and Clawsuss. It couldn't a been so long before I downed him, either. And I didn't want to make no mistake about riddin' the world of Butcher Krantz, so I crocked him one on the head. I heard his skull crack. And here he shows up like this."

"That's why you always told everybody around here you wasn't afraid of the Butcher," Mark divined abruptly.

"Well, you wouldn't be much afraid of a man you was damn sure was good and dead, would you? But I wasn't goin' around telling anybody I'd laid him out, and you can bet on that. A man like him always has some faithful followers that'd have it in for the one that bumped him off. So I kept it to myself. But believe me, I'm going to make good and sure I get him this time!"

"You can't hold Norman Symone to account for what Butcher Krantz done, Crook," Mark interposed swiftly. "I'll barge around and get hold of him and take him back to Hell's Gate. We'll be damn careful he don't get away again."

"Too late." Crook's face was grim and harsh. "He may have been without his memory before, but he ain't now. I couldn't understand the change in his face when he stood there starin' in the window, it's been puzzling me all along, but now I can sure see what caused it. He was lookin' for them nuggets, all right; I'll wager you're right as rain there. And he saw this back room with a light in the window, and came to see what I was doin' here.

"At first he just saw a man getting up from the table to leave the room, then he took a good look at me. I didn't even know him at first. His face looked kind of familiar, but I couldn't figure who he was and what he was doin' there. Then his face began to change. I know now what made it. He knew me. Who'd forget anything that looks like me? He knew he'd seen me before, and he stared, tryin' to recollect where. It came back to him, and everything else with it. He turned into a fiend again right there when I was lookin' at him. He seen the man what had give him that crack on the head, and then's when he remembered."

"Logical," Mark breathed. "Logical as hell. And it was you—you that so near done for him."

"And it ain't my fault I *didn't* put him under the dirt, either," said Crook shortly. "I sure tried hard enough. If I'd had any idea there was still any life in his hellish carcass I'd have slit his throat. This time I'll cut his damn head clear off! I'm gonna lay a trap for him, and he's gonna walk into it as pretty as you please."

"You're gonna do no such damn fool stunt!"

Mark contradicted sharply. "You're gonna come out to Hell's Gate with me, and stay out of his way. He's after you, or he will be, since he recognized you."

"Certainly!" Crook admitted with some vehemence. "And that's just why I'm stayin' right here and not budging a foot. It's why you're goin' back to Hell's Gate to-night."

"I am not!"

"You sure are!" Crook thrust forward his big head.

"I'm stayin' right here to help you—"

"You're doin' nothing of the kind! You're gonna stop bein' a bull-headed fool right here and now, and you're goin' back out there this evenin' and explain things to Clawsuss. He's got a right to know. When I sent for you, I intended to keep you here, but what you've told me kind of changes things. Think of Clawsuss! Pore devil, he'll be on hot needles till you get back and tell him what's what. That's one reason you got to go. The other is that I want plenty of protection out there for Jo-Anne and Petey. And they'll think they're safe, that far from Canyon Center. They may be out rambling all over the country. Tell 'em to stay in the house and keep it locked!

"There's just two places he's sure gonna go, Mark. As sure as hell he'll go back to Buckshot Canyon to see if he can learn who Clawsuss is and why Clawsuss took him out there to see those nuggets—then didn't produce the man that had 'em. That's the other reason you got to go back, and stay right there till we get him dead to rights. And if he shows up there first, you see if you can move as fast as you did the first time you showed up here."

"It took me a few years to learn to be that fast," said Mark steadily. "I reckon I can move one ahead of him."

"I'd judge so." A dry smile flitted across Crook's grim face. "The other place he's sure to visit again is here. That's why I'm stickin' close. I'm layin' a trap for him, I tell you, Mark. And he can kill half the town if he wants, but I'm not budgin' a step till he comes here to finish me off or somebody else gets him. No matter where he goes, or what he does, here's the one place I'm damn *sure* he'll come before he tries to leave town. Here's the one place where we can lay a trap and *know* we'll get him.

"It's going to be a water-tight trap, too, old timer! A little while after I sent Jo-Anne off to Hell's Gate, I sent one of the boys here to Saw Tooth Canyon for Single-Shot Andy and the whole damn Gang. They'll be gettin' in here shortly after midnight. Then we're gonna work fast. Right here is where the Butcher makes his last stop! There's eight men in The Gang. There's only one window in this room. We'll work shifts of four, four all day and four all night, so no matter when he comes we'll get him. Four of The Gang will be hid within sure fire, surrounding the approach to that window, every hour from to-night on."

"And you?" asked Mark.

"I'm the bait in the trap," said Crook dryly. "I'm makin' me a bed down on the floor over there in the corner, so I can even sleep here. And when he sneaks up to the window to see if I'm in here alone, four guns will let him have it to once. Every man in that Gang is a dead shot. I'll have the light burning strong all night. So day or night, when he steps up to that window he'll be a perfect target. And four dead shots will let him have it, every man shootin' at a different vital spot. I'd like to see the man who could survive that much lead poisonin'!"

"Sounds air tight, Crook," Mark admitted. "You're sure usin' your head. But we better not sit around this room too much till The Gang does get here, I reckon. I'll lay down pretty soon and knock off an hour's sleep, if you don't mind. Then I'll line out about midnight for Hell's Gate. Kind of keep you company till then. The Gang ought to be showin' up before that."

"Pretty close to it," agreed Crook. "Sure, you can go over to my room and sleep any time you feel like it." He rose from the table and gestured toward the saloon. "Come on in and have another good cool schooner before you turn in."

Mark slept five hours and returned to the Happy Daze, where he drank another round or two of beer with Crook, and they left the saloon to the tending of Pete Cobalt while they repaired to the back room to talk things over. Crook said he was taking no chances till the men from Saw Tooth Canyon came in, so he and Mark sat there talking with lowered voices in the dark, with only the white moonlight showing dimly through the window. It was the sanest strategy, Crook said, and went on:

"If he comes sneakin' around to-night, he'll see the room dark and go on. He'll show up later for business when he sees a light burning. I'm makin' no light in this room till I get Andy and the boys here."

Mark commended the sagacity of his brother, and when it neared midnight he went out to saddle his horse with a feeling of relief and security regarding Crook. Not even Butcher Krantz could get away from the trap being laid by Crook and the Saw Tooth Canyon Gang. Crook bade him good-by with an air of grim satisfaction and settled determination.

"You folks all stay close out there at Hell's Gate, and don't worry about me," Crook admonished, in parting. "Butcher Krantz has come to the end of his bloody trail. When it's all over, I'll let you know."

CHAPTER XXI
HORROR

MARK made better time going home than he had in traveling to Canyon Center the day before. He reached Buckshot Canyon a couple of hours before noon, to find Clawsuss alone. Garner Blue and Petey were out roaming around somewhere with Satan. Petey never tired of the wonders of the canyon. Jo-Anne had taken Clawsuss' mining pan into an adjoining gulch and was striving to wash out some gold to see what it would feel like to separate the precious metal from the earth with her own hands. Mark's first word was a question as to the whereabouts of everybody else, and he frowned in uneasiness when Clawsuss told him where the others had gone.

"We'll have to round them up and get 'em in here," he said. There was a reluctance about him, a hesitancy, as if he feared the very words he was forced to say, hated the sound of them and was driven to speech only by the utmost necessity. "They ain't exactly safe away from the house. The bars and locks you put on this house to hold a man in, I'm afraid, are going to come in handy to keep him out."

Clawsuss had been sitting brooding in a chair when Mark came up the steps. He had straightened, erect and alert as Mark entered the room. Now he rose slowly to his feet and his dark face paled in dismay.

"Yuh mean—it really was the Butcher Crook saw?"

"It was seein' Crook that turned him into the Butcher again," Mark explained baldly. "All I can do is to tell you just what Crook told me." And he proceeded to do it. "It's a hell of a thing to have to tell a man about his own brother. I've been tryin' to imagine all the way home how I'd feel if it was Crook. But that's one thing no man could imagine very well, I guess. I couldn't blame you for anything you'd do. I wish there was something I could say to make it sound less ugly."

"There ain't nothin' no man kin say," Clawsuss replied harshly. "Things is as they is. Only—I could wish that Crook had made a better job of it when he tried tuh finish him in Californy. I'm goin' out and bring Jo-Anne in. I know just where she is. You go round up Garner and Petey. Yuh kin leave the tellin' of 'em tuh me."

In less than two hours all the dwellers at Hell's Gate were within doors, and Clawsuss told them without preamble what Mark had learned concerning the truth of the reappearance of Butcher Krantz.

"Butcher Krantz and Norman Symone are the same man," he said in conclusion. "Crook Alvord was the man that hit the Butcher on the head and knocked all the meanness out of him. He tried tuh kill him, and thought he did. That's why he was never afraid of Butcher Krantz showin' up, like everybody else was. It was seein' Crook himself that brought the Butcher's memory back. As Crook told Mark, there's just two places he's *shore* tuh go afore he tries tuh leave town. That's tuh the Happy Daze—and here. We're all gonna stay close and sit tight till we hear from Crook.

"Dealin' with a halfway sane man wouldn't be so hopeless. But nobody that has the impulse tuh go around slashin' people up thataway kin have much sanity in them. Gawd knows where he ever got such a streak. It never was in his father or mother, nor in none of the rest of us."

Jo-Anne echoed the one word involuntarily, under her breath, *"us!"* Clawsuss looked at her steadily, with eyes that were stark in a colorless face.

"He was my younger brother," he said, using the past tense as if the Butcher were already dead.

Jo-Anne turned a tragic horrified gaze on Mark. "Oh, Mark! What—what are we going to do?"

Mark stepped closer to the chair where she sat and laid one hand reassuringly over the hand she had half instinctively reached out toward him. "There ain't nothin' anybody can do. That's the hell of it. For your safety, and Petey's, we have to do what Clawsuss says, set tight till we hear from

Crook. Don't go to worryin' none. You're safe here, no matter what turns up."

Safe? Jo-Anne knew that she was, wherever were Mark Alvord and his deadly guns. She glanced covertly at her father, and he caught the look. Killer he had once branded Mark Alvord. And she had replied that some day they might be glad of that fact. Blue nodded slowly, answering her unspoken thought. It was as if he had said, "Yes, you are right."

The remainder of that day was a difficult interim for all of them. Yet an outsider watching their casual attitudes would scarcely have realized that they were people ridden by suspense and horror, each striving continually to conceal the fact out of consideration for the others. All moved by the same impulse, they retired early. None of them to sleep, but Petey was the only one that had solace. Jo-Anne patiently told him endless fairy tales to comfort him because he had had to stay in the house all day. It was late before any of them fell asleep.

Clawsuss was last awake, but he finally dropped to sleep also, only to be startled suddenly awake again. He woke with the consciousness that it was well after midnight, and that he had been for some time sound in slumber.

He sat up in bed, with the feeling of having heard an unusual sound, listening to ascertain what had startled him. The night was still. Only Mark's regular breathing at his side came to his straining ears. Then abruptly he heard Satan growl, ominously, warningly. He leaped out of bed, went into the big living room and called up the stairs.

"Yuh stay there, Satan!" he commanded curtly. "Stay there, and keep still."

Instantly the sound that had wakened him was repeated, and he knew it for the same sound the moment it came again. It was a sharp rap on the heavy door leading to the porch. Clawsuss stepped close to the door and spoke in a lowered voice.

"Who's there? And what do yuh want at this time of night?"

"It's me, Clawsuss. Red Regan." The answer came in urgent, excited tones. "Let me in quick. I got to see you right away."

Clawsuss scowled, starting toward the door in the darkness, and turned his head as he heard the sound of Mark Alvord sitting up in bed.

"Wait till I slip into my pants, Regan. It's purt' nigh freezin'. Then I'll let yuh right in."

The giant hurried into the bedroom, struck a match and lit the kerosene lamp on the window sill. Alvord, blinking his eyes at the light, shaking the sleep from his brain, stared at him, startled.

"What's up, Clawsuss?" he asked, suspicion narrowing his gaze, and apprehension sent a chill down his spine.

"Can't tell yet." Clawsuss slipped into his trousers, buckled on the single-shot pistol, picked up the lamp and started for the other room. "Regan's outside sayin' he's got to see me right away. Sounds pretty much het up, too. I reckon yuh better git yore clothes on."

He hurried on into the other room, placed the lamp on the table and hastened to admit Regan. As the door swung open, the miner rushed into the room, jerked himself to an abrupt halt and caught the giant's arm. It was an excited man that faced Clawsuss. His face was pale and haggard, his red hair in a disheveled thatch over his narrow eyes.

Clawsuss gave one look into his face and let out a startled ejaculation. "Whut's the matter, Regan?"

"Hell's a-poppin' in Canyon Center!" Regan announced swiftly, his gaze holding Clawsuss as he covered the situation with concise words that jabbed into the giant like the blade of a dagger. "Somebody killed Crook Alvord in the back room of the Happy Daze, last night. Of course, everybody knowed Mark was in town, but the murder wasn't discovered till after he was gone, or he'd never got away! He—"

"Hold on!" Clawsuss cut in harshly, thinking of Mark, standing in the adjoining room and listening to every word. "Are yuh tryin' tuh tell me them fools in town think, because Mark said what he did when he first come and made up with Crook— they think it was Mark who shot him?"

"Shot?" Regan returned sharply, his face paling to a ghastly yellow as he recalled the grisly scene he had looked upon in the back room of the Happy Daze saloon. "He wasn't shot! He was cut to ribbons with a knife! God, he's an awful sight! Everything points to Mark. He was there all day with Crook. Pete Cobalt and all the boys seen him go into the back room with Crook, after supper, and them two was in there all evenin'. We heard Mark ride away along about midnight. Crook didn't come back into the saloon, and we thought it was kinda funny at the time, but nobody said anything. Pete thought maybe he had gone to his room.

"Then, just when we was gettin' ready to leave, here comes Single-Shot Andy and the whole damn Gang, all lathered up from ridin' hell bent to town because Crook had sent for 'em and said it was a matter of life and death for 'em to get there quick. Pete went into the back room to see if by any chance Crook was still there. The light was out, but Pete struck a match to see if Crook had left things in order. The back door was standin' wide open. Crook was still there all right. I—I couldn't bear to look at him."

"Christ, Regan! Are yuh tellin' me Crook's killed, cut up like that, and they think Mark done it? Mark never did! Maybe what this town's been afeared of for so long has come tuh pass. Maybe that's—*maybe that's the work of Butcher Krantz!*"

"By God, it sure looks like it!" Regan returned violently. "But man, what *else* would it be? That's why Crook had sent for The Gang. He musta knowed the Butcher was gonna break loose. And he knew somethin' none of the rest of us knowed—he *knew who the Butcher was.*"

Clawsuss cut in with a furious, indignant cry. "Yuh ain't insinuatin' that they think *Mark's* the Butcher?"

"What else *can* they think?" countered Regan harshly. "Crook wasn't never afraid of the Butcher, eh? Good reason why! He thought even the Butcher wouldn't jump his own brother, I guess. But he musta made Mark mad, and Mark musta threatened him—because Crook got scared as hell and sent for The Gang—too late."

"Mark never done it, I tell yuh!" Clawsuss retorted savagely. He wheeled and called through the door leading into the bedroom. "Mark, come out here!"

Alvord appeared in the doorway, fully dressed, his guns at his belt. His eyes were terrible, his mouth was drawn into a straight ugly line, his gaunt face a pasty gray.

"Yuh never killed Crook last night, did yuh?" Clawsuss demanded, his eyes boring into Mark's.

"Hell, no!" Mark's gaze swept contemptuously over Regan, and leaped back to the giant. "And any man who thinks I did is a sneaking skunk not fit to live! Crook was my brother, and he had growed to be my friend. And it's me that's gonna git the white-livered coyote that carved him up!"

"Then you better be movin'!" Regan warned darkly. "Half the town's on the way out here to get *you!* Nobody knows you so very well in town, Mark. We ain't seen so much of you since you come. All hell couldn't make 'em believe you didn't do it."

"They'll believe it when I get the Butcher who did do it!" Mark snapped.

"And not until!" Regan turned abruptly to Clawsuss. "They don't nobody know I took a horse and hit the trail hell-for-leather to warn you, Clawsuss, only Pete Cobalt. He sent me. If everybody didn't like you so well, and if you hadn't always been so square with everybody, I'd never a come. But I don't want to see you getting into no mess on account of Mark and what he's done."

"Hell'n Blazes!" snapped Clawsuss, his voice ugly. "Didn't yuh just hear Mark say he never done it? Let 'em come. I'll handle 'em. Reckon the fools is bringin' a rope?"

"Bringin' a rope and all the guns in Canyon Center!" Regan answered curtly. "And you can argue yourself blue in the face, Clawsuss, but it won't do no good. They may listen to you, but they'll never believe you, and you can't stop 'em. They think all that play Mark made of being friends with Crook was just to put Crook off his guard till he got a good chance at him. You better beat it, Mark! They'll show up here in a coupla hours howlin' for blood. I'm gonna git, right now!

Never do for 'em to find out I warned you. They'd string me up for it before I could say half a dozen words. They're plumb crazy mad. Everybody liked Crook. But you guys better get busy. They're comin' fast. Better take to the hills, Mark. I'm gone!"

Regan wheeled, slipped out the front door and slammed it behind him.

For a moment there was a dead ugly silence in the cabin, then Clawsuss turned slowly to face Mark Alvord. Both men wore colorless, expressionless masks, behind which lurked tragedy and rage and death. Swiftly Mark cut into the unbearable silence, voicing the thought that had turned the blood to ice in their veins.

"You reckon things is as black against me as he made out?"

"Sounds like it," Clawsuss replied hoarsely, and knew Mark's thought. Both of them had harbored the hope that Butcher Krantz was gone into oblivion for all time. Both of them fought an overwhelming surge of horror, in which their rage and instant resolve to avenge Crook battled with a dismaying shock at the preposterous thought that had taken hold of Canyon Center. What ghastly irony, that men should think Mark was the Butcher. "But how yuh suppose he ever got in there?" Clawsuss stumbled. "After all the precautions Crook took."

"He musta been layin' for him," Mark returned. "Right there close. When I left, we went out the back door, and Crook was standin' by the barn when I rode off, intendin' to return through the same door."

"Gawd!" Clawsuss cut in. "And the Butcher was layin' fer him there in the dark when he come back. Prob'ly had been cached there most of the evenin', waitin'."

"I reckon," Mark agreed. "He coulda heard the sound of voices in there if he'd been close, although he couldn't have heard what we was sayin'. If—only I'd a stayed till Andy and The Gang come. But I was so sure he was safe."

"It—it's hell, ain't it?" There was inarticulate rebellion in the giant's voice. "But I reckon—I reckon when them fools from Canyon Center gits cooled down a little I kin make 'em see light and set 'em lookin' for the man that *is* the Butcher."

Clawsuss set his teeth grimly, and Mark stepped close, his gaze boring into the dark, tortured face.

"See here, Clawsuss. We got to snap outa this. We got to do just one thing. We got to remember! You got to remember Cass Greggory, and I got to remember Crook! I got to ask you something, and you got to think hard before you answer. If *my* brother killed *your* brother, what would *you* do?"

Clawsuss went rigid, and his eyes narrowed sharply at the sudden thought that shot under Mark's words.

"If anybody killed my brother," he answered evenly, his voice dead and his face blank, "I reckon, regardless of who that killer was, I'd go after him. Brother is a awful strong word. Father's a kind of strong word, and mother's kind of holy soundin', and sister's real nice and friendly like. But I reckon there ain't no word that's got the guts and bindin' power that brother has. Shore as your breathin', Mark, I'd go after the killer. And I'd go to git him!"

Mark stood motionless, holding Clawsuss' gaze, his face harsh and his eyes grim. There was no mistaking the thing Clawsuss meant. He was viewing clearly the fact that Butcher Krantz was his brother. And he was telling Mark to go get the man who had killed Crook. And each knew that the other was also seeing the fact that if Mark got the Butcher, Krantz was still the giant's brother. Clawsuss had said "regardless of who the killer was." Brother was a strong word!

Mark's sallow face was the color of bleached parchment as he answered, "Crook was my brother." He stood straight as an oak, and his voice was hard with utter lack of feeling. "You and me swore to be pals. Reckon we'd always be pals at bedrock no matter what come. Till hell froze over. That's been my creed. Well, hell's froze. And I'm goin' outa Hell's Gate to git me a pair of skates and take a fresh start!"

CHAPTER XXII
PARTING OF THE WAYS

As Mark wheeled and turned into the bedroom to secure his mackinaw and hat, a stir overhead gave evidence to the fact that Jo-Anne had wakened and was aware of something unusual in spite of the fact that the men had guardedly kept their voices lowered. Clawsuss started as her call came down to him. He had utterly forgotten Jo-Anne Blue. Their voices had been lowered not out of consideration for her, but because they spoke of things that are not shouted at the top of the voice. He turned his head to catch what she was saying.

"Clawsuss! What's the matter down there?"

"Why, nothin', ma'am." The giant forced the casual words from a stiff throat, as he stepped to the foot of the stairway. "At least, nothin's the matter here."

"I thought I heard Satan growl." Jo-Anne's voice came from the hall, and Clawsuss knew that she had risen, crossed the room and opened her door the better to hear what he said. "But he didn't make any more noise, and I was about to go back to sleep when I heard you and Mark talking. There isn't anything wrong, is there?"

"Yes'm, there is," Clawsuss answered quietly.

"Somethin' pretty bad has happened and there ain't no use tryin' to keep it from yuh. Yuh better git dressed and come downstairs. Yuh got to know about it, and the sooner the better, I reckon."

He heard her gasp of dismay as she hastily closed her door, and the spat of her bare feet hurrying across the floor. At the same instant he heard Mark's footsteps entering the living room from the bedroom, and he turned back to face him with grim eyes.

"I—I got to see her—before I go," Mark said, haltingly. Clawsuss nodded and turned away. He walked to the far end of the big living room and stood with his back toward Mark, staring out the window into the night. Both of them heard Jo-Anne come hurriedly down the stairs. She saw Clawsuss' rigid figure at the window, saw Mark's gaunt, pasty face.

"Mark!" she went swiftly toward him. "Mark! What is it? You look terrible!"

"I *feel* terrible." He caught at the hand she laid on his arm, and shot one desperate glance at Clawsuss' rigid back. "Red Regan came out to warn us. The Butcher killed Crook last night—and they think I done it."

"Oh—Mark! No! How perfectly terrible!" She tried to repress the involuntary cry, but it escaped in spite of her.

"Yes. I—got to get out of here."

"But Crook knew the Butcher had shown up,

Mark. He saw him through the window. No—Mark! They *can't* think *you* did it!"

"But you got to remember nobody else knew Crook had seen the Butcher," Mark reminded her. "It don't look very pretty for me. Crook sent for Single-Shot Andy and The Gang, but he only said for them to come quick, as it was a matter of life and death. Crook was killed not more than ten or fifteen minutes after I left. They know I was in there with him all last evening. They think the Butcher has showed up, all right, but they think I'm the Butcher."

Jo-Anne went quite white, then she stepped close, and her other hand gripped Mark's other arm. "*You* the Butcher? Oh, the fools! The utter fools!"

Mark smiled wryly. "But they think it, and from where they sit they got good reason to think it—and they mean business. They're on the way out here now, after me. And I have to go, only—I guess I thought I could fight it out easier if I knew you believed in me."

Jo-Anne's face quivered and the quick tears stung her eyes. "Believe in you? Oh, Mark. You surely didn't think I could doubt you?" Her slender hands, gripping his arms, shook him impatiently. "Didn't you know any better than that?"

Mark's lead-gray eyes glowed. "Thanks Jo-Anne. I reckon that was all I needed. I'll slug my way through, somehow, now."

"You shall! You have to. Because all the time you'll have to remember that I'm here waiting for you to come back." Before he grasped her intent she raised herself to her tiptoes and kissed him squarely on the mouth. "You *have* to come back."

"Well, by God, I will!" Mark swore.

He turned from her as Clawsuss swung about and advanced toward them. He knew that every moment counted. No time was to be lost.

Not a word was said between the two men as they walked to the heavy front door. With expressionless faces they stood for a moment eye to eye. Suddenly Clawsuss thrust out his hand, and Mark gripped it convulsively. Then Alvord wheeled, jerked open the door and vanished across the porch in the blackness of that hour which precedes the dawn. Clawsuss closed the door, locked it and turned back into the room. Jo-Anne came slowly toward him, her hair hastily braided and her hands fumbling nervously at the throat of the dress she had donned. She caught the giant's arm in a tense grip.

"Clawsuss—Clawsuss! I think I'm frightened out of my head."

"No'm." His eyes flinched from her face and dropped to the head of the huge dog that had followed her downstairs. His gaze came back to Jo-Anne's face steadied, unflinching. "No'm, I reckon yuh ain't quite. Yuh got to git a grip on yoreself, Jo-Anne. Yuh got to remember yo're in the West, and they's lots of things happens out here that ain't right pleasant. Yuh got to remember that they's a lot of fellas on their way out here to git Mark. But they ain't gonna find Mark here."

Jo-Anne fell back a step, her hand raised help-lessly to stifle the cry that rose to her lips, her eyes dilated in horror. "But—how can they ever think Mark did it?"

"They don't know him like we do. Lots of inno-cent men gits in bad thataway. Yuh see, ma'am, we gotta be cool headed and realize that they's some things looks bad for Mark. This here what yuh call circumstantial evidence. Mark never would have laid a finger to Crook. Him and Crook was right fond of each other. I knows he never killed Crook, and I knows jist what makes things look like he did. But that bunch of fellas headed out this way is crazy mad. Everybody liked Crook—and I reckon I'm gonna have a lotta trouble makin' 'em under-stand that Mark never done it."

"Oh! What are we going to do?" Jo-Anne shiv-ered, frightened temporarily into a state of panic.

"We all got to do a lot, ma'am," Clawsuss answered, holding her eyes steadily. "Yuh listen to me, now. Yuh got to buck up, Jo-Anne. The only way to keep them fellas from stringin' Mark up to the first tree after they catch him, is to git the fella that killed Crook and git him quick! Of course, Mark's already gone out to try and round him up now. But Mark can't do it all. I got to go, too. I hate to leave yuh, but yuh'll be all right here with Garner and Satan tuh protect yuh, if yuh'll jist do what I tell yuh. Will yuh?"

"Yes, certainly." Jo-Anne's hardy spirit rallied to the tone of the giant's words, to the very words themselves that demanded her courage, as she would have rallied from a fainting fit at a dousing of cold water. The panic went out of her eyes, and her pale face set into lines of cool control. It was a hideous thing that had happened—and it had happened to Mark! She righted herself abruptly, threw back her shoulders and looked into Clawsuss' eyes with valiant readiness to face anything required of her. "What shall I do?"

"You stay right in this house and don't go out fer anythin'," Clawsuss commanded, relieved and gratified at her quickly regained poise. "I'm goin' toward town and head off that crowd of crazy galoots that's comin' after Mark. I know I can't stop 'em from beatin' over every foot of nigh territory lookin' for Mark, and I can't send 'em back to town. But I can hold 'em up for a while and give Mark plenty of time to git out of their way, and I can stop 'em from botherin' you."

"I'm not afraid of them," Jo-Anne returned quietly. "They wouldn't harm me."

"No'm, they wouldn't. But I ain't gonna have 'em worryin' yuh none. I'll give 'em my word that you three is alone here, and they'll believe me, and do as I asks when I say to let yuh alone. But yuh see here, Jo-Anne!" Clawsuss stepped close to her and looked sharply into her eyes, striving to impress her with the importance of his request. "No matter what happens don't yuh go outa the house for nothin'. And don't yuh let Satan out. Keep the doors shut and locked, and try to take it easy. Don't let nobody in but Mark. Here—wait a minute."

The giant turned and strode into the bedroom adjoining, returning immediately carrying a heavy Colt .45 which he laid on the table.

"I'm leavin' yuh that gun. I don't reckon yuh'll need it none, but yuh never kin tell."

"I understand." Jo-Anne's eyes returned his gaze with a steadiness that made him exult in the thoroughbred grit of her spirit. "I'll lock the doors and admit no one but Mark."

"Maybe yuh won't need the gun," Clawsuss answered quietly. "But I'm leavin' 'er anyways. There she is, all ready to spit. Yuh don't need to cock the hammer. All yuh got to do is pull the trigger. But don't pull it none unless yuh mean business. She barks pretty easy. Now I'm off. Yuh ain't gonna fergit nothin' I been tellin' yuh, ma'am?"

"No. I'll not forget. I—I was upset at first, but I'm all right now. Go right ahead. It's a terrible thing that's happened to Mark. His brother! You've got to go. No one with any spirit would want you to act otherwise."

"Yes'm. You—yuh're right spunky, ma'am. I shore admires yuh for it."

Clawsuss turned away and again hurried into the bedroom. Jo-Anne stood leaning against the table, listening to the sounds from the room adjoining. The rasp of a match as he struck it to light a candle. The heavy sound of his feet as he moved about gathering up one thing and another. Shortly he returned to pause before her, a heavy mackinaw pulled up about his ears to battle the raw chill of the morning air in the deep canyon, his hat jammed down over his cold eyes. He gestured toward the stove across the room.

"The fire ain't gone out yet, and there's plenty of wood in. Yuh kin keep plumb comfortable. And see here, Jo-Anne, don't yuh go to worryin' none if Mark don't show up afore I git back. Yuh jist take care of yoreself and be as patient-like as yuh can."

The giant started toward the door and Jo-Anne stretched out a hand to detain him. He paused, glancing at her in slight surprise. Her eyes held his, softened with emotion. Suddenly, in the crisis, she realized to what an extent had grown her warm regard and liking for the giant of Hell's Gate.

"Clawsuss—you'll be careful? We've come to think a lot of you. It would be very terrible if anything should happen to you in this hideous affair. You'll be careful?"

"Why—why, yes'm. Shore I will!" Clawsuss stumbled over the words, confused and delighted at the warmth and concern for him that her manner revealed. Shyly he raised his big hand and held it toward her. "Shake on it! We been learnin' to think a lot of you and Petey, too. Good-by, ma'am. I'll be back—quick as I kin."

She walked with him to the door, unlocked it and flung it wide. Outside the first gray light of the morning had crept into the canyon, pushing back the blanket of shadows till only ragged tatters of the night lurked between bowlders and trees. The giant stepped out on the porch, pulling his mackinaw snugly about his ears, and Jo-Anne smiled after him.

"Clawsuss—luck go with you! And come back quickly!"

"Yes'm." Clawsuss turned to glance over his shoulder as he went down the steps. "Keep Satan close, ma'am. Take—take keer of yoreself."

Then he was gone, walking swiftly through the morning shadows, toward the barn to secure Ripp. Jo-Anne closed the door and locked it again, reaching to pat the head of the huge Dane, feeling a sense of security in the house this man had built, guarded by his dog.

She smiled to herself as she thought of his confusion at her friendly warmth. Parting. There was something about this parting that touched the hidden depths, as parting always does. It bore so much on Mark Alvord. She realized that the world would seem oddly blank without Mark.

CHAPTER XXIII
THE BITTER TRAIL

OUTSIDE the house Clawsuss hurried to the barn, saddled and bridled Ripp in the stall and led him out into the raw dawn. As he swung into the saddle he glanced toward the house, where the light shining thinly through one window reminded him of Jo-Anne's presence there.

The giant's dark face held rigidly straight ahead as he rode past the cabin and turned into the trail that led to Canyon Center. Without conscious thought his right hand strayed to finger the single-shot pistol he carried at his belt, then rose to ascertain that the ugly automatic rested securely under his armpit. Nearly an hour later, riding briskly along the trail, Clawsuss raised his bent head to see the advancing mob from Canyon Center riding toward him down the canyon.

They were incited enough because of their shock and horror of the night before to be in an ugly and murderous mood, to listen to little reason, but he rode on toward them calmly, his mind working in swift and logical sequence. They halted in a concerted, jostling crowd at sight of Clawsuss astride his big brown gelding. The giant drew Ripp to a halt and scrutinized them silently, sweeping his hard eyes from face to face.

"Where's Mark Alvord?" demanded Peck without preamble.

"I don't know," Clawsuss returned quietly. "He went trailin' the man that killed his brother."

"Hell's bells!" shouted a man behind Peck. "He killed Crook hisself and you know it!"

"That's a lie!" Clawsuss snapped out the denial, and the men in the mob went still. "I don't know nothin' of the kind, no more'n you do. Yo're all jumpin' to conclusions jist because Mark told it honest that he come out here to kill Crook. But he meant what he said when he made it up with Crook, and they got to thinkin' a plumb lot of each other. And yo're all of yuh mighty pore judges of men if yuh think Mark would be guilty of such a ugly job as that that was pulled in the back room of the Happy Daze!"

"Oh hell!" Peck cut in hotly. "All that play he made to win Crook's good will was just to put Crook off his guard. He's been mighty slick about it. Givin' us all time to fergit what he said when he first come here, and waitin' till he got a good chance at Crook. He even fools you with his smooth tongue. But he ain't fooled us. Maybe you don't know that Crook sent for Single-Shot Andy and his Gang, because he was scared of his life!"

"Where *is* The Gang?" Clawsuss demanded.

"Beatin' the woods about town, to be sure Mark don't get by in that direction."

"Yo're crazy!" Clawsuss snapped. "Mark never done it!"

"Well, it's damn sure nobody else done it!" the man behind Peck retorted harshly. "He tried to be pretty slick, playin' us along that way. Then when he thinks we forgot all about it and everythin's jake, he comes into Canyon Center and butchers Crook somethin' awful—and you let him get away! Clawsuss, you got to tell us where he went!"

"I don't know!" Clawsuss reiterated, eyeing the crowd steadily, playing for time. "He just strapped on his guns and went."

"But look here, man!" Sanders Lee crowded into the front row of the mob, a triumphant leer on his face. "If Mark didn't tell you, how the hell did *you* find out Crook had been killed? And don't it seem kinda funny to you that Mark'd come clear out here to Buckshot Canyon just to tell you he was goin' after the man who killed Crook? He was plannin' a smooth getaway. Slick right down to the last play!"

"He never knowed Crook had been killed for hours after he come home." Clawsuss looked from one man to another thinking swiftly. His first reply to Peck's question had admitted knowledge of the killing. It was dangerous to let them think Mark had reported it himself, but shield Regan he must. "I can't tell yuh who brought us the news. But a man who's my friend came and told us about Crook. Mark was as shocked as me. He dressed and lit out. I knowed of no reason for stoppin' him. He was doin' what I'd have done. I'm on my way right now to help round up the man who needs killin'. Yuh better turn around and beat it for town with me."

"Not by a damn sight!" Sanders Lee thrust out a pugnacious jaw, and his eyes narrowed. "Mark's as slick as they make 'em, but we'll get him before he legs it out of these hills. We're not going back to town with you. Think we're gonna risk *Butcher Krantz* slippin' away from us? We're going straight down the canyon, and we're going to find Mark Alvord before we do any turning back. Get out of the way, Clawsuss. We don't want any trouble with you, but we're sure going to get that butcherin' Mark Alvord. There wasn't another man in town who had any reason for killin' Crook, and you know it! Crook didn't have an enemy to his name!"

"Well, yuh stay away from Hell's Gate!" Clawsuss ordered peremptorily. "I'm givin' yuh my word that Mark ain't there, and that's enough. Garner Blue's there with Petey and Jo-Anne. She's all upset about Crook, and I left Satan to take care of her till I git back. Don't go round thar shootin' of yore faces and worryin' her none."

"All right, all right!" agreed Peck impatiently. "We wouldn't bother Jo-Anne any more than you would. We ain't after women and kids. We're after the dirty coyote that butchered Crook Alvord, and we're goin' till we git him. Out of the way, Clawsuss!"

Impatient ugly muttering rose in the crowd back of Peck. Clawsuss realized that he had held them in check as long as was humanly possible. But Mark had had a good two hours' start, and there wasn't much danger of their catching him anywhere. Silently the giant pulled Ripp to the side of the trail and allowed the angry, cursing mob to sweep by him. He frowned after them, his dark face sinister and his eyes narrowed shrewdly.

If he figured rightly, the man who had killed Crook Alvord had never headed back toward Buckshot Canyon, but had certainly gone the other way. Mark, with the same idea in mind, would swing out in a wide arc, pass Canyon Center and close in. Clawsuss would ride straight through Canyon Center, and keep on going, and between them they would bring their man to bay. With a curt order to Ripp, he urged the big horse into a swinging gallop on the trail to Canyon Center.

CHAPTER XXIV
I AIN'T GOT A BROTHER

PETE COBALT, owner of the Happy Daze saloon, stood behind the bar, his chin dropped on his chest, his moody eyes watching through his brows the three men who were conversing in low

188

tones at the end of the bar. He could hear nothing they said. Their words were lowered in deference to him. Pete had liked Crook, as everyone had. He knew they were talking of the murder. Murder was an unusual word in Canyon Center. In that wild little town a killing was simply a killing, common enough in the demands of justice, and seldom rousing resentment against the killer.

Plenty of men who needed killing drifted in and out of Canyon Center. But Crook Alvord had not been one of them. And this was no ordinary affair of rough justice, where a skunk had been laid low for some rotten deal, or one man had been downed by a better man in self-defense. This thing had no roots. For no reason at all someone had murdered gay, irresponsible, bullnecked Crook Alvord; had murdered him wantonly, hideously mutilated his corpse. And since Crook was unanimously liked and had no enemy, there was but one man who could logically be suspected of the crime. Vengeance! was the infuriated cry, thought, and curse of Canyon Center.

Pete Cobalt looked up as a shadow fell across the doorway. To the figure entering the saloon, he voiced a quiet greeting. The three men at the end of the bar ceased talking, to nod to the giant who was distantly friend to every man, and to shoot frowning glances and grimaces at each other. Clawsuss was as wholesalely liked as Crook had been, and Clawsuss was Mark Alvord's acknowledged pal. They watched unobtrusively as Clawsuss paused at the bar and returned Pete's grave, subdued greeting, refusing his invitation to have one on the house.

"Afternoon, Pete. No, thanks, Pete. I ain't drinkin' right now. I been all over town in the last hour; now I wanta see Crook. Where is he?"

"Oh." Pete's frown deepened, and a look of nausea whitened his mouth. "Sure, you can see him if you want to. He ain't a very pretty sight, Clawsuss. Come on inta the back room. We ain't took him outa there yet. Sheriff Keene didn't want we should move him for another day yet."

"Say—Keene!" Clawsuss leaned over the bar struck with a sudden thought. "That's right. The sheriff wasn't with the crowd I met headed for Buckshot Canyon. Where is he?"

"Why, he took a handful of men and went the other way, in case Mark had streaked off in that direction. Most of 'em thought he'd head for Buckshot, but Keene wasn't taking no chances on missing him. He sent somebody out in every direction. But—what you wantin' to see Crook for, Clawsuss?"

"Jist want to see if I kin rake up any clew you fellas mighta missed."

"Ain't no clew." Pete started down the bar, beckoning Clawsuss to follow. "Not a one. Not a thing laying about. The knife that was used on Crook ain't lyin' around anywhere. Keene wouldn't let nobody go in the room and disturb the body. But you can step just inside the door and look, like everybody else did. Can't do no hurt."

Clawsuss followed him around the bar, his thoughts racing. If Keene had sent men in all directions, some of them would be certain to pick up Mark. His eyes were mere slits as he stepped into the back room halting just inside the swinging door and waiting as Cobalt leaned inside, to pull back the blanket covering Crook and to raise to his feet with face averted.

Clawsuss had looked on many dead men. He had seen the work of Butcher Krantz. But what was left of Crook Alvord, the mutilated thing on the floor that had been the man he had known and liked, was so ghastly a spectacle that he involuntarily took a step backward. The work of Butcher Krantz. There could be no doubt. Clawsuss' face was pasty as he jerked his horror-fascinated eyes from the hideous body on the floor and flashed them at Cobalt.

"Gawd! Pore old Crook. We shore has got to git the man that sliced him thataway!"

"Well, where is he? Don't you know?" Pete asked sharply.

"Damnit, man!" Clawsuss snapped. "Yuh ain't fool enough to really think Mark done that, are yuh? I know he didn't! I—I *know* who the Butcher is. But it ain't Mark!"

The dilated pupils of Clawsuss' eyes glowed a

sultry red, like the eyes of a mad dog. The anger on his dark face caused Cobalt to suppress an involuntary shiver. No longer were the giant's thoughts chaotic. This knife-riddled body at his feet had been the brother of his pal. Butcher Krantz was behind this slaughter, and the Butcher must pay. Clawsuss of Hell's Gate had no brother.

The stamp of feet and the clamor of angry voices bursting into the saloon startled Cobalt and the giant from the tense tableau in which they stood. Cobalt sprang to the swinging door and shoved it aside to look into the room. At his sharp ejaculation of astonishment Clawsuss wheeled, leaped to look over his shoulder and shove into the room. The huge man's voice boomed out in enraged bellow.

Mark Alvord stood against the bar, eleven threatening angry men crowding him close, eleven men composed of the three who had already been in the saloon and eight others. Single-Shot Andy and The Gang. Mark's flaming, dangerous eyes leaped to Clawsuss' face.

"What you fellas tryin' to do?" Clawsuss roared, striding up to the men with a belligerent scowl corrugating his dark face.

"We're rounding up the dirtiest skunk that ever came to this town!" snapped Yellowjacket Bevans.

"How'd it happen, Mark?" Clawsuss asked swiftly.

"I was riding around the town to see if I couldn't

head in on him," Mark returned. "And these guys nabbed me like a lot of damned fools and dragged me into Canyon Center."

"Well, I found out all we need to know," Clawsuss eyed Mark steadily, emphasizing the words that would make clear his meaning to Mark but be utterly incomprehensible to the other men. "I seen Crook. He ain't a healthy sight. And listen—yuh hear me, Mark? We reckoned we wouldn't know when we'd meet ag'in nor how. But the trail's clear for both of us. *I ain't got a brother!* You *had* one, and we're goin' after the butcher that killed him—you and me—together."

Mark's face could go no whiter, but it turned a dirty, sickly yellow. He understood. All that was left in the giant's brain was the old cry for vengeance in Cass Greggory's memory, wiping out all of the ties of blood in the name of justice.

The crowd of men around Alvord bunched closer, threatening, cutting into the silence with menacing oaths.

"Not by a damn sight, you ain't! Alvord ain't goin' outa town, Clawsuss. He ain't goin' nowhere! Sheriff Keene sent us out to git him, and we got him. And we're not letting him out of our hands. We're holding him till Keene comes back— unless we decide we can't wait for Keene and string him up ourselves."

"You're right!" A burly man with a heavy, anger-reddened face turned toward Clawsuss, his hand wavering suggestively toward the gun at his belt. "There's eleven of us here, and eleven guns that says Alvord stays right where he is."

"We got to demand justice, regardless, Clawsuss," Single-Shot Andy said curtly. "You can go where you please; but we've got Alvord, and we're hanging on to him. You better stay out of this, man!"

"Yuh better stay out of it yoreself!" Clawsuss warned grimly, but Single-Shot Andy interrupted his further speech and dropped his hand to the butt of his heavy Colt.

"Somebody's gonna get hurt if you persist in buttin' in, Clawsuss! We'd do a damn lot for you, and you know it. We even ain't got nothin' against you for being fooled by a slicker like this Butcher. Yuh can argue all day, but we're sure as hell gonna hold Mark Alvord!"

"Reckon yo're talkin' too fast. Don't make me mad, Andy!" Clawsuss whipped out the single-shot pistol and covered the men, backing to the bar and menacing them with his red-lit eyes. "Mark never done it, and if yuh won't take my word for it yuh'll have to take what's comin' to yuh. I'm gonna take care of Mark till we git the guy who killed Crook. He's goin' back to Buckshot Canyon with me as quick as we can git there. I got one shot here. The first man as makes a move gits it. And after that I got plenty more. Mark—where's yore hoss?"

"Out in front," Mark answered evenly. "But

man, you better give in and leave me here. You can go on and get him, and all you got to do is get him here and prove his guilt to Keene in time."

"Yo're goin' with me!" snapped Clawsuss. "These crazy fools'd string yuh up the minute I was outa sight. Pete!" Cobalt answered tersely from where he still stood by the swinging doors. "Yuh go out and git Ripp and Nigg and lead 'em around to the back door. Leave the door open. And—Pete—pull that blanket back over Crook. Move, will you, Pete? I'm givin' yuh my word that I *know* Mark never done it—and I know who *did*. That Mark *ain't* the Butcher and I know who is. And I'm not stoppin' for nothin' till I git him. Now, move!"

The swinging door squeaked slightly as Pete turned and pushed through it. Clawsuss again addressed the crowd around Mark.

"You gents back away from Mark. I drill the first man as don't do as I say! Back!" Cursing, furious, watching for the slightest chance to drop the giant, the men moved back from Alvord. "Mark, come here." The thud of horses' hoofs came into the room, as Mark obeyed and sidled down the bar till he stood shoulder to shoulder with Clawsuss. "Go on through the back room and git in the saddle while I hold these fools," Clawsuss ordered. "Ride up the trail till yo're out of sight and wait there for me. And—when yo're goin' through the back room—don't look on the floor."

Mark, disarmed by his captors, and helpless to do otherwise, disappeared into the back room. In the same instant Single-Shot Andy whipped his gun from its holster and fired. Clawsuss' single-shot barked as the Colt roared. The bullet from the single-shot pistol spatted harmlessly into the wall. The Colt had fired the fraction of a second first. Clawsuss started like a man stung, the pistol dropped, and he swayed on his feet.

"Now we got yuh!" shouted another man in the crowd, his hand leaping toward his gun. "Try tuh reload that peashooter and I'll drill yuh!"

They had reckoned without Mark Alvord. In that back room he had seized Crook's guns. It had taken him but a second to whip aside the blanket that covered Crook, to snatch Crook's revolvers and leap to Clawsuss' aid. He appeared in the door now, both guns leveled, the hammers raised, and his voice challenged them. "Drill and be damned!" The look on his face would have daunted men more doughty than they. A concerted gasp of surprise swept over the crowd, and the hand of the man who had voiced the threat halted halfway to the gun it sought. Keeping them covered, Mark backed to the swinging door. "You fellas is too slow to think fast. Can you make out to follow me, Clawsuss? And you, Andy, you fellas listen: I got enough bullets here to send you all to hell, and I'll do it if you make a move."

"And yuh listen tuh *me!*" Clawsuss put in, his right hand clamped tightly against his left side, the blood already beginning to ooze through his fingers. "I mean what I told Pete! I know for a certain fact that Mark never killed Crook. Did any of yuh ever know me to lie to ary man?"

The crowd of faces stared back at him dumbly.

"Answer me!" he snapped.

"No. None of us ever did, but this is a hell of a funny way for you to be actin'."

"Nothin' funny about it! I'm just savin' a innocent man from a pack of crazy fools till we git a chance to git the fella that really needs killin'. I'm askin' yuh to not say nothin' to Keene or nobody else about where Mark is. I'm goin' his bond. I'll see that he don't go nowhere that I don't go till we rounds up the man what killed Crook. I tell yuh I know who the Butcher is—and it ain't Mark! Will yuh keep yore mouths shet and give a man half a chance?"

"Maybe. We ain't promisin'."

"Well, we're gone," Mark warned grimly. "But if you go and tell Keene and bring some more men out to Buckshot Canyon, you're runnin' inta Hell's Gate—and you wanta remember that! And there'll be lead spittin' for every man of yuh! You better stay in your own back yard!"

Alvord stood motionless, guns still on the angry baffled men, as Clawsuss backed through the open door beside him, across that back room and on out

197

the back door. Then in a whirl of swift movement Mark followed. As he swung into the saddle the men came boiling around the corner of the saloon, and they came ready to shoot. Mark dug his heels into Nigg's flanks and turned in his seat, both guns out. But none was ready to provoke the weapons of the man they still believed to be Butcher Krantz. He leaned low over Nigg's neck and passed from sight into the trees lining the trail that led from the rear of the saloon.

A few yards ahead he came up with Clawsuss. He greeted the wounded man grimly. "We got to work fast. The whole town's hog wild. You ain't hurt bad, are you?"

"No, not too bad," Clawsuss answered. "They won't listen to no sense, will they? They won't believe nothin' I say. They think I'm jist tryin' to shield you. We got to git to Hell's Gate. Gawd!"

"What's the matter?" demanded Mark.

"I jist got a sudden idee! I got a idee that cain't fail! Ride, man! Ride fast, and ride straight! I jist thought up somethin', somethin' that plumb cain't fail. Ride!"

CHAPTER XXV
THE WORD OF A MAN

As Clawsuss and Mark thundered out of sight, Cobalt turned to the crowd of cursing, angry, baffled men.

"Come into the saloon and have a round on the house," he invited, his voice tense and his eyes surveying them swiftly. "Come on. I'll set 'em up. I want to talk to you."

The men turned back into the saloon, cooling a little at the surprise of Pete's generosity. They wondered a trifle what had got into Pete, but Pete wisely forbore to enlighten them till they had rounded up before him in the main room. Then Cobalt leaned over the bar and demanded their attention.

"Listen, men," he requested impressively. "I've got something to say to you. Clawsuss is telling the truth. We've all known him too long to doubt that. He's certain in his own mind that Mark had nothing to do with the killin' of Crook."

"Hell! Mark just put one over on him. He's slick!" protested one of the men hotly, banging down his glass on the bar.

"That may be so. Clawsuss may be mistaken. And again—he may not!" Cobalt held their attention persistently. "He may be right. He's so sure he knows who killed Crook, I vote we give him a chance. Maybe he *does* know the Butcher. We got no right to be so certain it's Mark just because we never see him before, and none of us knowed the Butcher by sight. Give Clawsuss a chance!"

"Yeh, and let Alvord slip out on us!"

"Not by a long shot!" contradicted Cobalt. "Didn't Clawsuss say he'd stay right with Mark? He ain't hurt bad. He'll keep his word. He won't let Mark get away. If he discovers that he's wrong, and Mark did do it, he'll turn him over without a word. But we'd feel mighty sorry if we strung up Crook's brother and found out afterward that somebody else *had* butchered Crook. Do you think there's a man of you liked Crook any better than I did?"

"No—no, I reckon not," Single-Shot Andy admitted soberly.

"Damn right you reckon not!" Cobalt shot back vehemently. "And there ain't a one of you more anxious than me to see Crook's murderer get it in the neck. But I vote we give Clawsuss a chance. He give us his word, and it's the word of a man."

Cobalt's liquor and Cobalt's clearcut argument was having its effect on the enraged men who had been cheated of their prisoner. They were cooling fast, and the saloonkeeper pressed home his advantage swiftly.

"Give Clawsuss two days to find his man. I'm like all the rest of you. I can't think of a fellow anywhere who had any motive for killing Crook Alvord. But maybe Clawsuss knows of one. Anyhow, give him a chance. Keep your mouths shut for two days. Nobody'll think of looking for Alvord at Hell's Gate now. The rest of the fellows are out in the hills looking for him, and they ain't likely to give it up and come back before to-morrow or next day. You guys just keep shut that long, and if Clawsuss don't come through we'll take the whole damn town and head for Buckshot Canyon. We'll go for Mark Alvord and we'll get him if we have to set fire to Hell's Gate! Are you with me?"

Abetted by his powerful whisky, Pete Cobalt won the day. The men finally gave in, although they did so rather reluctantly. One by one they swore on their word of honor to remain silent about Alvord's whereabouts for two days, to give the giant of Buckshot Canyon time to make good his word to them. Cobalt cursed under his breath in fervent relief, filled them up again and told them the last barrel was the limit. He alone, of all the men in the saloon, thought of Norman Symone, the stranger who had been guest at Hell's Gate. Single-Shot Andy and The Gang considered the poor halfwit too wild a chance to be entertained as a possibility. Clawsuss had mentioned no names but Cobalt wondered secretly what old feud Clawsuss might have unearthed between Crook Alvord and the stranger he had been entertaining at Buckshot

Canyon. The stranger was the one man he could imagine as being inimical to the murdered Crook, as possibly being the Butcher, and that merely because he believed every other man in the town had liked Crook unreservedly.

As the men in the saloon quieted to grumbling, still-protesting argument and speculation, Cobalt slipped again into the back room, where the mutilated Crook lay again hidden under the blanket, and stood staring down at that concealed figure, the ghastliness of which was still clear before his eyes. Had he made a mistake in abetting Clawsuss, that mysterious man none of them really knew? Should he have, rather than using every effort and idea to hold the angry men in town, urged them to follow the giant to Hell's Gate, to prevent any miscarriage of justice? For an instant, shuddering at the thought of Crook's terror and pain in that grisly struggle before death mercifully released him, Cobalt was half inclined to whirl back to the other room and send the men charging upon Buckshot Canyon.

But Cobalt was cool in the head, quick in the brain and just in the heart. He had to remember that Clawsuss was, and had been ever since he had known him, a man to drill straight toward justice, fearlessly and honestly, no matter whom it might hurt. No—better not go to doubting a man whose word had always proved twenty-four carat, Cobalt concluded.

And Clawsuss *had* been utterly sincere, that much was certain. Cobalt felt himself chill afresh at recollection of the look on Clawsuss when he had seen that mutilated corpse. Was it possible, though, that Clawsuss had also seen some other seemingly inconsequential thing that, though it might appear insignificant to others, was a clear clew to him?

Cobalt braced himself inwardly for the sight, bent over and lifted the blanket gingerly, and studied long the body of Crook, the disheveled, torn clothes, the floor close to the figure. Nothing was there in which he could see the slightest cause for suspicion. He dropped the blanket back, and turned away.

As he went slowly from the room, Cobalt reminded himself that he had always wondered why a man like Clawsuss was isolating himself there in Buckshot Canyon—why he wore that queer alias—why he had built such a strange house—why he so consistently avoided too close contact with other men. There had always been a good many other things to wonder about Clawsuss. That witless Symone, for instance. The stranger again intruded into Cobalt's disconnected thought. Funny thing, that. Clawsuss, lone wolfing it for years, then suddenly taking on Mark Alvord. And shortly afterward inviting the newcomer Symone to come to make an indefinite stay at Hell's Gate.

More than funny, strange or queer! Cobalt

started as he abruptly remembered something the dead Crook had told him some time since: how, the first time Clawsuss and Mark Alvord had appeared in Canyon Center, somebody had mentioned casually the arrival of Symone in Saw Tooth Canyon, and how Clawsuss had been violently agitated at sound of the name, then had curtly denied any knowledge of Symone. *Then had invited the man out to his cabin.*

Cobalt swore to himself. The mystery of the lone giant of Hell's Gate was about to be solved—and the stranger Symone was the key to the riddle.

"Holy Cripes!" Cobalt muttered under his breath. "I wonder if that Symone can be the Butcher?"

He stood for a moment shaken by the whirl of sudden thought that engulfed him, then the cool head and just heart got on the job. Whatever the answer, the battle was Clawsuss'—his to settle the score, and the best thing Pete Cobalt could do was keep his mouth shut, his eyes and ears open, and wait for the storm to break.

But—Symone! And another strange thing occurred to Pete Cobalt. Several men had been there the night of which Crook had told him, had seen the agitation of Clawsuss at mention of Symone's name. Queer nobody else had thought about it.

Then a last bewildering query tugged at Cobalt's confused brain:

"By God! If it *was* Symone, *what the hell did he want to kill Crook Alvord for?*"

CHAPTER XXVI
THE SOMETHING
THAT COULDN'T FAIL

IT was breaking another dawn when two horses, lathered and weary, loped into Buckshot Canyon and drew up before Hell's Gate. Mark reached for Ripp's reins and motioned Clawsuss toward the house. As Clawsuss swung out of the saddle, Mark ordered tersely, "Go on in and tell Jo-Anne we're here. She'll git some hot water and clean up that side of yours. I'll put up the horses and be right in. Half the town's still headed up the canyon somewhere lookin' for me, and I got to work fast, like I said. But you got to take it easy. You've lost too damn much blood already."

Clawsuss turned toward the house and walked difficultly up the four low steps. Before his hand could touch the panel, the door swung open and Jo-Anne faced him, all dismay over his condition, all eagerness to aid him. She saw the blood on his hand and on his shirt and her concerned eyes flashed to his weary face.

"I saw you coming, Clawsuss. I've been watching for you all night. Who did that to you?"

"Single-Shot Andy, ma'am. But he wan't tuh blame. Everybody's all het up over this, and don't rightly know what they're doin' nohow. Mark's all

205

right. He'll be in as soon as he puts up the hosses." Clawsuss glanced swiftly around the room. "Whar's Garner?"

"Upstairs trying to put Petey to sleep with fairy stories. The poor little fellow is so restless, having to stay in the house like this. But don't stand there talking about Petey! You're hurt. Sit over here by the fireplace. I have a kettle of hot water on the stove. I'll get it. Don't you move till I come back."

She left him sitting in the chair before the fireplace, while she hurriedly fetched hot water and bandages, removed the rough bandage he and Mark had applied on the way out from town; and as she dressed his wound she talked on. "All those men came by here searching for Mark. They looked at the house pretty sharply, but none of them made any move to stop. Wait—there's Mark now." Jo-Anne turned with a sigh of relief as Mark entered the room. "Mark! I'm glad you're back. Did you— did you—" she faltered and stumbled, unable to finish the grim question.

"No'm." Mark shook his head as he closed the door behind him. "We didn't catch him. But we're going to. Clawsuss thought of something. And you ain't told me what it is yet, Clawsuss."

The giant's dark face was pale with the beginning of weariness; but its pallor deepened as his thought leaped back to the thing he had remembered as he and Mark rode out of Canyon Center. He had remembered suddenly the night that Garner Blue had grimly remarked he'd hate to see Satan go after any man he wouldn't want to see killed.

"I'm tellin' yuh now," Clawsuss replied. "They say there ain't no real clew to who killed Crook, only circumstantial evidence. I reckon they're makin' a mistake. There *is* a clew. But a man cain't git it."

"What you talking about?" Mark asked sharply, and Jo-Anne stared at the giant with startled eyes.

"The scent of the man that killed Crook is in that room," Clawsuss replied, his eyes never leaving Mark's face. "Of course, there's been other men in there since, but not many, and it's plain that Crook and that fella fought all over that room afore he finally got Crook down and out. That fella's scent'll be stronger than any other in there, and it's still fresh enough for a dog to git it. Well, a dog's gonna git it!"

Jo-Anne cried out and hid her face in her hands at the giant's unmistakable meaning. His face went ghastly, but not once did he look at her. Desperately his gaze held to Mark's gaunt, pasty features.

"What's the idea?" Mark cried out. "You ain't meaning—"

"I ain't meanin' nothin' else. Yuh trained Satan tuh kill, and yuh trained him tuh trail, didn't yuh? Good! That's all we need. The fella that killed Crook has got far enough away so that they'll never catch him in any ordinary way, or else he's stickin' right around here thinkin' nobody'll ever suspect him. Ain't I right?"

Mark nodded in agreement. Jo-Anne shuddered and dropped limply into a chair. The giant went on evenly, still not taking his eyes from Mark's face; "Well, we got to git him, and we got to git him quick. I know of jist one way of doin' it. I'll have tuh stay here with Jo-Anne. You git that cap in my room, the one Norman left on the bed. Let Satan smell it—then take him to the Happy Daze and see if he kin ketch the same scent in that back room. If he can—let him go!"

Mark and Jo-Anne stared at him in dumb horror as he turned his head to call the big dog. The Dane rose at his command and stalked up to him. Clawsuss' gaze turned again toward Mark, but it avoided the woman huddled in the chair. Mark knew that the giant was close to the end of his tether.

"I'll git me a bite from the storeroom," Clawsuss' voice came muffled and difficult. "Then I think I better lay down for a stretch. I'm thinkin' maybe Pete Cobalt'll do what he kin to hold them crazy fools up a while. Pete knows me. But you lose no time, Mark. Go with Mark, Satan! Git a move on yuh!"

Jo-Anne flung out a deterring hand as Clawsuss started to rise. "You sit still, Clawsuss. I'll get whatever you want to eat." She rose and followed Mark to the door of the bedroom where he had gone to get the cap left behind by Norman Symone. As he came out of the room, the cap stuffed in his pocket, she stood there waiting for him. He stopped short, a warming light flashing across his face.

"Mark—" Jo-Anne held his gaze with eyes that pleaded for assurance. "You'll have a care what you do, won't you? You're entering upon such a dangerous mission."

Mark laughed, a short grim laugh, with a queer little note of exultance deep in it somewhere. "You think they could get me when you're here waitin' for me to come back?"

"You needn't be afeared fer Mark, ma'am. That boy kin take keer of himself." Clawsuss spoke from his chair. "I think, Mark, yuh better help me tuh bed afore yuh go. I'm feelin' kinda dizzy."

Jo-Anne turned swiftly, and both she and Mark hurried to Clawsuss. He got to his feet with difficulty, and, one on either side, they helped him into his room and onto his bed.

"Maybe you'd better go get him something to eat," Mark suggested to Jo-Anne. "And some hot strong coffee, plenty of it. I'll get him into bed."

Jo-Anne turned away without a word and hurried into the kitchen to replenish the fire and put on the coffee. She was still busily preparing Clawsuss' food when she heard the sound of the front door closing. She listened for a moment, then put down her work and half ran into Clawsuss' room. Mark was not there. Jo-Anne caught her breath, feeling a little empty sensation in her breast.

"Clawsuss! Has Mark gone?"

"Yes, ma'am." Clawsuss turned his head to look up at her. "He didn't want tuh say good-by. Don't yuh worry about him, none. Yuh oughta seen the way he set The Gang on their ears after Andy winged me. He kin keep his own hide whole, and don't yuh go doubtin' it."

Jo-Anne did not answer. She heard the clatter of Mark's horse's hoofs as he rode by the cabin on his way back to Canyon Center. Then she became aware of Clawsuss' gaze, and her eyes rested on his colorless face. She felt a wave of contrition, that she should have been thinking only of herself.

"Oh, Clawsuss. How horrible—how perfectly horrible all this is for you!"

"Yeh. Yes'm." Clawsuss nodded, watching her dumbly. "But I reckon it's just as horrible—for some others. Ma'am, we got to buck up and hang on. Mark is doin' the only thing a man can do. I want you to allus remember that, and never hold nothin' aginst him. Anybody that goes around cuttin' people up thataway has got tuh be stopped. And if Satan kin find him, I reckon Satan'll do one thing that'll make it worth while his havin' lived!"

"Why, I'm not blaming Mark!" Jo-Anne's eyes widened in surprise. "Of course he's doing the only thing a man can do! He's got to get that horrible murderer somehow! Oh—I forgot!"

"That he's my brother?" said Clawsuss grimly. "Well, he ain't—not after what he's done. I ain't got no brother."

Jo-Anne turned her head, listening, at the sound of feet on the stairs. "Here comes Dad. That means he's got Petey asleep. I'll send him in to stay with you while I finish getting your lunch ready."

CHAPTER XXVII
MAN HUNT

IT was not until he was well on the way to Canyon Center that Mark Alvord allowed himself to think. They were thoughts of such wormwood and gall, so compounded of rebellion, bitterness, fury and compassion, that he dare not think them in front of her. But now, they raged and tore, and not even Mark Alvord could repress them.

Wide or closed, his eyes saw everything repeated over and over—like transparent pictures superimposed one on the other—that rumpled blanket lying upon the floor in the back room of the Happy Daze, with a hump under it: a hump that was all that was mortal of the brother he had lately found, only to lose. Crook—the Durham-faced old galoot; he'd been all right. And now he was dead. Hideously dead. By the Butcher's knife. That Satan would track the killer was inescapable. Satan wouldn't fail. And he, Mark, would have to see

Clawsuss' brother torn and mutilated to death before his eyes, rent by Satan's slavering jaws.

Mark clenched tight his smarting eyes and shut his teeth on a moan of agony.

"God! What a hell of a place to be in! But what could I do? I got to go, and it's only justice. The Butcher's got to be stopped. But—the dog *I* trained —and *his* brother. After the way he's been to me. Plumb hell and nothin' less,—but what must it be to him?"

Mark set his teeth on a fearful curse. He didn't know there was such a word as Gethsemane, but he knew quite well what it meant.

Jo-Anne Blue, crouched on the foot of her bed, hearing her father pacing the floor so restlessly and so wearily, shuddered and wished she could sleep, and wept a little for Clawsuss' anguish—and suddenly wondered why he should request her to hold nothing against Mark. An odd thing to ask. But perhaps he feared that it might seem a hideously brutal thing to her, his taking that mean dog to hunt down the murderer. She had to admit that, even though she liked him, Satan could be awful enough.

But of all of them, entering to that dreaded Garden, none was now so completely horror-ridden or without hope as Clawsuss, lying weakened and light-headed because of his wound. Not the least of his distress was his inner turmoil over the evolution of the Butcher. And he was savage with anger that his wound had laid him low and prevented him from traveling with Mark in the service of justice. He visioned Mark, gaunt and solitary, following the big dog indefatigably, with that spirit which can know no rest till its objective is achieved.

As for Mark himself, it was late afternoon when he flung off his horse in front of the Happy Daze, left the spent, sweat-lathered horse standing, and rushed into the saloon. Pete Cobalt stood behind the bar, and four men who had been in the crowd that had taken Mark were drinking at the farther end of the bar. Otherwise the saloon was empty. Cobalt looked up and emitted a sharp ejaculation as Mark rushed into the room, the big dog at his heels.

"Is Crook still here?" Mark demanded abruptly.

"Yeh." Cobalt nodded studying Alvord's gaunt haggard face. "But Keene's gonna take him out today. Got to. Where's Clawsuss?"

"In bed. A damn sick man from that lead Andy threw into him," Mark returned shortly. "Is Keene back?"

"Yeh." Cobalt nodded. "They're all pilin' in, fagged out and mad as hell. I talked the fellas inta keepin' their mouths shut, though. They're giving you two days. What you want?"

"I want to see Crook again." Mark leaned over the bar and fixed Cobalt with hard, steady eyes.

"And I want to borrow yore big roan horse. My brute's all in. I been riding hard. Listen—I'm explainin' to you. We ain't got no clew, only circumstantial evidence, and you all think I done this job just because it looks that way. But we all overlooked a bet. We got a clew, but it takes a dog to follow it. We got the scent of the killer—it's on the floor, the furniture, it's all over the room. I'm sending Satan after him. I want your horse to follow Satan with."

"By Cripes!" Cobalt swore softly. "Well, you can sure have him. But ain't Satan already tired out, from the trip in?"

Mark shook his head. "I carried him in on my saddle most of the way, to keep him fresh. Had a time of it, even though the brute's trained to ride in a sling. Does he look tired?"

Cobalt looked down at the massive Dane. "No, by God," he swore. "Jed!" And he wheeled to address one of the men at the bar. "Hike out to the barn and toss Mark's saddle onto Smoke. Move! Come on, Mark—see if Satan can get a scent."

He started down the bar as Jed Roper hurried out to saddle the roan. Mark called the dog and followed Cobalt into the back room. He strode to the body, partly pulled aside the blanket and called the dog to him. Then he took from his pocket the cap he had brought.

"Satan, yuh got to git somebody! Look here!" With a steady hand he pointed to the cap, his narrowed eyes commanding the huge dog. Satan stood rigid, staring first at the cap then at the dead man, whining, hackles raised, long tail held out straight behind. At Mark's repeated order he edged close and leaned to sniff over the gray cap. Mark rose to his feet and stepped back. "Snoop around and see what yuh can find. *Git him!*"

For a moment the dog continued sniffing at the cap, then slowly and carefully he began weaving back and forth, sniffing Crook's mutilated body from head to foot. Back and forth he walked, pausing to smell intently at certain spots, then weaving on again. Suddenly he dropped his muzzle to the floor, followed some scent across the room to the window, down again to the floor, back to the body, then to the outer door. There he reared on his hind feet, pawing at the wood and whining sharply.

"He's got it!" Mark cried excitedly. "Satan! Come here!" The dog obeyed with manifest reluctance, glancing toward the door, whining and growling deep in his throat, as though he were gnawing at a bone, pausing at Mark's feet to stare up into his face with red gleaming eyes. Mark patted a hand on his chest. "Come up here!" The dog reared to his hind feet and placed his front paws on the broad chest in the very spot the patting hand had indicated. Mark took the dog's great head between his hands and stared into the animal's eyes.

"You'll know that fella when you find him, won't you? I wonder can you understand what I'm saying to you. Go git him! You hear me, Satan? *Git* him! Sic 'em! *Go git him!*"

The Great Dane glared intently into the man's eyes, his own lurid pupils glowering like globes of phosphorus. Suddenly his long hard-muscled body went rigid and still. His lips writhed back from his bone-white teeth in a snarl. He growled deep in his throat, a murderous, menacing growl that made Cobalt's flesh creep. Mark pointed a steady hand at the door. Without taking his eyes from the dog's, he spoke to the saloonkeeper in a low aside.

"Pete—open the door."

Cobalt crossed the floor and flung the door wide. "Satan! *Go git him!*"

The dog dropped to all fours with another snarl, leaped across the room and dashed out the door. The two men rushed to the open doorway to watch him. Jed had brought the big roan horse around the corner of the saloon, and stood quietly by the saddled animal, interestedly taking in the scene. Again the dog began weaving back and forth, now between the door and the trail, his nose close to the ground. Then suddenly he found the scent, winding off through the trees to the left of the trail down which Mark and Clawsuss had escaped the day before. With a sharp whine, the Dane struck off at a lope. Mark sprang to the roan and swung into the saddle.

"Wait!" cried Cobalt. *"Whose cap was that?"*

Mark eyed him coldly. "It belonged to Norman Symone."

"Symone!" Cobalt echoed and remembered his own deductions.

"Symone!" reiterated another voice, and Single-Shot Andy appeared in the door of the back room behind Cobalt. "Yuh mean tuh say Norman Symone's the Butcher?"

But Mark had whirled the roan and dashed away to follow Satan. Single-Shot Andy wheeled upon Cobalt.

"Is that what he meant?" Single-Shot demanded. "That Norman Symone is really the Butcher?"

"Satan found Symone's scent in there." Cobalt gestured toward the back room. "You can do your own figurin', Andy. But it looks to me purty conclusive proof that we've been after the wrong man."

Andy shook his head slowly. "I don't know as it proves jest that," he said dubiously. "It does prove that there's a damn strange mixup of some kind out there at Hell's Gate. We've all of us been lookin' for somethin' tuh break ever since Clawsuss come out tuh Saw Tooth Canyon and took Norman Symone away with him. Ever since that day we've all been certain that Clawsuss was the big man named George that Symone's been lookin' for, and that more'n likely Clawsuss knows more about that flask of nuggets than he chooses tuh tell. But I

217

reckon, till we sift this thing down and see what's what, we ain't lettin' Mark Alvord nor any other man take complete charge of affairs in any such high-handed fashion."

"Well, what the hell you gonna do about it?" asked a voice behind Andy, and he and Cobalt turned to see Horse-Pistol Mike and the rest of The Gang coming around the corner of the saloon. They had not cared to follow in Andy's footsteps and pass through that ghastly room where Crook lay. Andy answered without hesitation.

"We're gonna git on our horses and follow Mark. How do we know that was Symone's cap he had? I never saw Symone wearin' no cap. Of course, that's no sign he never had one. But I've jest got a hunch I wanta be damn certain Mark ain't pullin' no smooth stuff. That guy's a killer, if there ever was one, and I ain't takin' no chances on him. Everybody move! We're ridin'!"

As the men rushed back around the saloon to get their horses from the hitching rack, Cobalt spoke to Single-Shot Andy rather sharply.

"You better put a little check on that trigger finger of yours, Andy. I'm afraid you've gone and done some purty misdirected shootin' already. Whoever Clawsuss is, and whatever the whole mixup, there's one man who ain't no murderer."

"But he may be willin' tuh shield a murderer." Single-Shot's reply was curt. "And him a friend of Crook—enough friend of Crook that I don't believe he'd be shieldin' Crook's murderer unless the murderer himself was a better friend and a man he thought more of than he did of Crook. By God, Pete, there's a lotta angles tuh this thing. And I ain't wantin' tuh make no mistakes."

"You already made one," Cobalt reminded him.

"I did not!" Andy retorted hotly. "I coulda killed him jest as easy, but I didn't want tuh kill him. I hated even tuh have tuh hurt him, but I had tuh get him out of the way, tuh clear the track for the rest of us, so we could be damn sure justice was done—*whoever* the Butcher was proved tuh be."

Andy was interrupted by the men of The Gang riding around the corner of the saloon to join him, to take Mark's trail. Horse-Pistol Mike was leading Andy's horse. Single-Shot strode toward his mount and swung into the saddle, waving a hand at Cobalt in a perfunctory salutation of farewell.

"Well, we're off, Pete. Don't go stewin' around and gettin' yore dander up. I ain't treatin' nobody tuh a dose of lead poisonin' less I know he's got it comin'. I thought yuh knowed me better'n that, Pete."

Cobalt laughed shortly. "You're purty hot headed, Andy. Mark Alvord is a dead shot and a dangerous man to trifle with."

"So am I," retorted Andy. "Come on, Gang, we're wastin' time. Pour the steel to 'em and let's see how fast we kin overtake Alvord."

The Gang swung into full speed down the trail

Mark Alvord had taken, and Pete Cobalt stood staring after them. He was remembering several things Crook had said to him after Mark had come, remembering Crook's delight in having things squared with Mark at last. And he knew something he couldn't make any other man see—he knew the look there had been in Crook's face several times when Crook spoke of Mark and Clawsuss. Whatever strange tangle wrought into complexity the lives of Mark Alvord, the Butcher, Clawsuss, Crook and Norman Symone, Cobalt was utterly convinced that Mark and Clawsuss were just and honorable men, as just and honorable as Crook had been. If any man in that group was the Butcher, he was ready to believe that it must be Norman Symone.

"And that damn fool hot-headed Andy is liable tuh go out there and raise some kind of hell that'll gum the whole works. Well—I don't know what I can do to stop it, but I don't know what harm could come from my bein' there, either. I think I'll just get astraddle of a horse myself and take the shortest road to Hell's Gate."

So Pete Cobalt saddled his horse and took the trail to Hell's Gate. But before he did so, he strapped on his guns for the first time in four years.

CHAPTER XXVIII
ALL ROADS LEAD
TO HELL'S GATE

ALREADY nearly a mile away from the Happy Daze, Satan drove steadily ahead, following the trail left by the Butcher, a trail that led him in a slight arc around the end of the town. Nose to the ground, ears sharply pricked forward, heedless of everything save that Mark was behind him, he followed the scent that was evidently still clear enough to give him a good lead. He came swiftly to the end of the arc where the Butcher had swung widely out, keeping under cover of the trees. There the trail swerved. Satan circled around several times, then suddenly picked up a clean scent, gave a short little excited bark and swung into his long lope.

With grim narrowed eyes, Mark followed on. As the miles fell behind, the dog traveled more slowly, till he had slowed to a fast walk. The afternoon waned, the sun dropped behind the hills, and the coolness of mountain evening began to settle. It was one of those evenings when the moon is already in the sky before the sun goes down, a gibbous moon, thin and white, seeming to grow in brightness and solidity as the darkness begins to fall.

Mark halted the dog, fed the animal and himself from the few remaining pieces of food he had packed into his pockets at Hell's Gate. He forced the Great Dane to lie and rest, while the horse grazed gratefully, saddle and blankets removed so that his back could cool. He turned the saddle over on its side, stretching the damp blanket across it, so that the dampened wool could dry and not be sodden with sweat when he returned it to the horse's back. Then he stretched upon the ground beside Satan, leaning against the back of the saddle, frowning and brooding, chafing over the necessary delay. Before he considered the animals and himself rested enough to continue the chase, it had grown quite dark and the moonlight had become very clear, so clear that every tree and bowlder cast a shadow, yet Satan's gray hide at even a short distance blended too quickly into the night to make him easy to follow.

Mark was of no mind to risk the dog's getting away from him. When he was ready to go on again he secured one end of his tie rope to the saddle horn and the other end to Satan's collar. And again on they went, over hills and down gullies. It was a wide territory before them, into which any man had open way and would be deterred by no obstacle. Mark's worry had been that the Butcher might have gotten too great a start on them. Every time the dog halted and lolled his tongue, Mark drove him grimly on with merciless determination.

"God, Satan!" he admonished the Great Dane more than once. "Move your stumps and let's git somewhere. The time's clickin' along damned fast." And the dog, recognizing that tone of authority only too well, stirred himself to greater speed and clung to the trail. Only at such times did Mark speak.

Otherwise he sat hunched and drawn-faced in the saddle, holding himself alert to cope with whatever situation hurled itself upon him when Satan should have cornered his quarry. So the strange silent chase kept up, steadily, till the moon had gone down, and the night turned black, and the first thin light of dawn told Mark that day was close at hand. But when that day broke enough so that Mark could see anything of his surroundings, his fear that the Butcher may have gotten too far away vanished and a new fear swooped down upon him.

The scent trail the dog followed had swerved. And now it cut straight across country toward Buckshot Canyon. When Mark saw that, his face went still whiter than weariness had made it. He was gifted with the power of visualization, which power may make a man very uncomfortable indeed at times. It made Mark very miserable now. He saw Jo-Anne, and Petey, and Clawsuss and Blue waiting there at Hell's Gate to hear some word from him. He saw the Butcher, sly and cunning as men of that type often may be, making his way to Buckshot Canyon and by some clever ruse gaining entrance to Hell's Gate. With a man like that anything was possible. He might make some hypocritical pretense of wanting to right things with his brother. For certainly, with his newly functioning mind, he could figure out that the brother George he had remembered from his childhood, the man who had been the partner of Cass Greggory, the owner of Hell's Gate and the man who possessed the nuggets were all one and the same.

Then, Mark reflected, striving to quell his own fears, Clawsuss wouldn't let the man in on any excuse, if Clawsuss were able to be out of bed and have anything to say about it; and Jo-Anne and Blue were both too frightened of him to allow the Butcher to enter the house no matter what plea he advanced, no matter what ruse he devised. But before he could draw a breath of relief, the most appalling realization of all swept down upon Mark Alvord. Few men who had ever known the Butcher for the Butcher had ever been allowed to live to tell it.

And Norman Symone would be fully cognizant now of the fact that Clawsuss of Hell's Gate, who was George Symone, his brother and mortal enemy, knew his identity beyond peradventure of a doubt. Mark raised his voice in a frantic curse.

"For God's sake, Satan, if yuh ever stretched those long legs of yours, do it now!"

For the scent trail, clearly and unmistakably was

driving straight toward Buckshot Canyon. And Mark visioned the Butcher arriving there, repulsed by those within the impregnable house, dynamiting the dwelling, or even setting fire to the sturdy structure of Hell's Gate.

"God'lmighty!" Mark groaned aloud. "*Anything* might happen. Satan! Move—damn your gray hide, move!"

At Hell's Gate, as the dawn broke, no one was astir but Jo-Anne and Garner Blue. Clawsuss, sleeping the drug-deep sleep of weariness and exhaustion, did not waken that morning till he heard Jo-Anne moving about in the kitchen and talking in low tones to her father. He lay there, inert, debating whether or not he should call to her, when he heard the sound of a horse approaching the cabin. He tried to sit up in bed, but he had not recuperated yet from the weakness caused by the loss of blood and he was forced to lie back again. The horse stopped in front of the cabin, a man's footfalls sounded upon steps and porch, and a rap rattled on the door. Clawsuss called loudly as he heard Jo-Anne coming cautiously from the kitchen in answer to that knock.

She heard him. Her footsteps halted in their swift light advance across the room and turned toward his door. The door swung back and she stepped across the threshold.

"I thought you were still asleep," she greeted

him. "I've been up for two hours. I hardly slept at all. I wish Mark would come."

"Who's outside?" Clawsuss demanded, his shadow-circled eyes burning and wide. "Sounds like half the town."

"It's Pete Cobalt, all by himself," Jo-Anne answered. "I saw him coming several minutes ago. I can't imagine what he wants, but I'll find out quickly enough. You lie still, Clawsuss, while I go to the door. I suppose it's all right to let Pete in?"

"Any time," Clawsuss answered without hesitation. "They don't make 'em any better'n Pete. But if Pete's out here all by hisself at this time in the mornin'—I reckon it'd be a good idea to let him in quick and shut the door behind him just as quick. And don't forgit tuh keep it bolted till Mark comes back."

"I couldn't forget, Clawsuss." She disappeared into the living room and the giant heard her walk to the outside door, unbolt it, and swing it open.

"Good morning, Pete," she said gravely. "You—you're out early, aren't you? Won't you come in?"

"Yes'm. It's kinda early all right." Cobalt stepped into the room and Jo-Anne swung the huge door quickly shut behind him, shooting the bolt and turning it before she gave him her attention. Cobalt went on rather hesitantly: "But I've just about *got* to see Clawsuss, if he can stand it to talk for a few minutes. How is he?"

"He's feeling very weak and worn, Pete. But he isn't very badly hurt. The worst of it was that he lost so much blood coming home. He must take things easy and keep quiet till he regains his strength. But I don't believe it would tire him to talk to you." Jo-Anne turned to lead the way into Clawsuss' bedroom, and Cobalt followed.

They entered the doorway to find Clawsuss lying motionless, his head slightly to one side, his eyes fixed on the doorway, waiting for them to appear. "Mornin', Pete," he greeted Cobalt quietly. "Has somethin' pretty bad happened? I reckon yuh better git it off yore chest if there has, and not keep none of us in suspense. We jist about had enough of that already."

"There ain't nothin' much happened yet that I know of, Clawsuss." The owner of the Happy Daze sat down in the chair at the head of Clawsuss' bed, and glanced inquiringly toward Jo-Anne.

"Yuh kin say anything afore Jo-Anne that yuh'd say afore me, Pete," Clawsuss answered the look. "I reckon I ain't got anything tuh hide from Jo-Anne."

Cobalt nodded. "I see. Well, it ain't much, you see. But—I kind of wanted to get here before anything *could* happen. Mark come into the Happy Daze yesterday afternoon with the dog, and he had a cap in his pocket, one that fellow Symone had had out here, he said."

"Yeh, that's right," Clawsuss assured him, holding his gaze steadily. "I told Mark tuh take it."

"Oh." Cobalt started slightly, but he went on without pause. "Well, he asked me to let him take the dog into the room where Crook was and see could he get the scent of the Butcher—from—from that cap."

"Well?" Clawsuss half rose in bed, his face drained of all color, and for a moment his eyes were half wild.

"He—found it." Cobalt did not flinch from the giant's vivisecting gaze. "He found it—and lit out after him. I asked him whose cap it was, and he told me. Single-Shot and the rest of The Gang showed up just then, some of 'em was already in the saloon when Mark first come. Single-Shot tried to ask Mark some questions, but Mark just beat it off after the dog, and Single-Shot braced me. You know how hot headed Andy is. I couldn't do much with him. He took The Gang and went off trailin' Mark. I thought you'd oughta know about things, so I—I saw to the buryin' of Crook and come straight here."

"Thank yuh, Pete." The wild light in Clawsuss' eyes had died, and he stared at Pete, and through him, not seeing him at all. "That was shore thoughtful of yuh. I ought tuh know all right. And I wanted tuh know. So—it *was* him all right. I didn't think there could be no mistake."

"Was him?" Cobalt echoed puzzled, made

uneasy by the look on Clawsuss' face. "Was who, Clawsuss?"

"The Butcher." Clawsuss' gaze came back from some remote spot and focused on the saloon-keeper's face. "I mean it was the Butcher who killed Crook—there wasn't anybody else did it."

"Hell no!" Cobalt stared. "Of course not! Nobody'd do a job like that but the Butcher. Who else did you think it could be?"

"Nobody." Clawsuss sank wearily back onto his pillow. "I *didn't* think it could be anybody else, Pete. I didn't even hope."

"Hope?" Cobalt repeated the one word in utter bewilderment.

Clawsuss nodded, his eyes wide and staring. Then even the stare changed to a look of settled resignation, and he turned a wry smile on Pete Cobalt. "Pete, yuh're a damn good guy. Crook would a swore by yuh any day, and I reckon I'm beginnin' tuh see why. We've allus been pretty good friends anyway, you'n me. Yuh must have had yore own ideas, didn't yuh?"

Cobalt nodded, attempting no deviation. "I kind of figured out who the Butcher was before Mark come in, Clawsuss. And I—remembered that you'n me had always been friends. It's none of my business what he ever was to you. I reckon there's a pretty bitter pill in it for you to swallow, and a man always feels for his friends."

Clawsuss glanced up at Jo-Anne. "I got some

pretty damn good friends, ain't I, ma'am? Would you tell yore dad to come here, please?" Jo-Anne nodded and went out of the room, and Clawsuss beckoned Cobalt to come close. "I didn't want tuh ask yuh afore her. She's pretty strong for Mark. But—was Andy and the boys still doubtin' of Mark and aimin' tuh cause him any trouble?"

"Oh, there ain't any danger of 'em ketchin' up with Mark," Cobalt evaded. "He and Satan had a long start on 'em. And even if they did, I don't think even Andy would be rash enough to do anything he'd be sorry for. The dog's gonna run down his man as sure as—" But there he heard the steps of Blue and Jo-Anne approaching the door, and he dropped the subject promptly. Both men were silent as the girl and her father came into the room.

Blue nodded at Cobalt, and paused by Clawsuss' bed. "What did you want of me, Clawsuss?"

Clawsuss looked up at him, then across at Cobalt. "Yuh know that big picture in the other room, the picture of the ship, mounted on a back made of boards and with the frame made of little twigs around it?" Blue nodded, and Cobalt said that he believed he had noticed it. "I want yuh tuh nail it to the wall," Clawsuss said. "It'd be kind of heavy fer one man tuh handle less'n he was jist takin' it down or somethin' like that. Garner, you git some nails and a hammer, good stout nails. Pete'll hold it for yuh—so it cain't slip. Nail it there so it'll stay as long as this cabin stands."

"Why certainly," Blue assented promptly. "Anything to be of service to you, Clawsuss. Come along, Pete. We've a job to do."

Cobalt followed the shoemaker out of the room., and Jo-Anne bent an intent gaze on the weary, white-faced giant in the bed. "Clawsuss! Nail the picture to the wall? What are you doing that for?"

He smiled thinly. "Ma'am, I'm closin' a book. That's all."

Jo-Anne nodded, and neither of them spoke as they heard the other two men moving about in the adjoining room, then heard the sharp steady blows of a hammer on big nail heads. There was no other sound anywhere in Hell's Gate, till the hammering ceased, and Blue laid the tool aside, to come into the room again followed by Cobalt, to announce quietly:

"She's nailed tight as anything could be, Clawsuss. Anything else we can do?"

"No—nothin'." Clawsuss looked up at Cobalt. "Thanks, both of yuh. I—I reckon yuh know too much, Pete, not tuh know more. Behind that picture is a iron box. In the iron box is a flask about half full of nuggets. He—he was my brother."

Cobalt bit back a startled oath. "God! And Mark—does he know it?"

"He shore does. He knowed it a long time ago." Clawsuss' deep eyes clung to the saloonkeeper's shocked face. "Don't make any mistakes, Pete. It was me who told him tuh take Satan and hit the trail. Brother's an awful strong word, Pete—but they's some things yuh cain't forgive, even a brother. And I reckon—I reckon I'd be much obliged to all of yuh if this never went no further. It's just one of them things that—that's—"

"It's a closed book," said Jo-Anne gently.

"Yes'm." Clawsuss smiled, a queerly grateful smile. "The book of judgment, ma'am."

"Well—" Cobalt cleared his throat uncomfortably, but whatever he started to say was destined to remain forever unsaid. The sound of horses and men came from the outside, a startled little silence fell over the room, and all of them looked at each other in inquiry.

"Single-Shot Andy and The Gang," said Clawsuss, "and I'll bet a hat on it. You go look, Jo-Anne, and if it's them tell 'em tuh come right in here, I wanta talk to 'em."

Jo-Anne nodded wordless acquiescence, rose from her chair and went hurriedly out of the room. Clawsuss had guessed accurately. Single-Shot and the entire Gang were waiting on the porch when Jo-Anne flung the door open and bade them to come right in, explaining that Clawsuss wanted to talk to them. They followed her into Clawsuss' room, surprised to find Cobalt there, but making no remarks about it.

"Mornin', Andy," Clawsuss grinned over at the big miner. "Yo're a bum shot. All yuh did was nick me."

Andy grinned back. Both knew equally well that the shot could have been fatal had Andy willed it so.

"Well, the best of us *will* slip up once in a while," Single-Shot assured him. "We come out tuh see if yuh'd heard anything from Mark yet."

Clawsuss gazed up at him steadily. "Not yet, Andy. But I'm lookin' for him any minute. I reckon yuh know by this time that Norman Symone was in reality Butcher Krantz?"

Andy frowned. "I reckon that's what we're here about, Clawsuss. Is he the man yuh meant when yuh said yuh knowed who the Butcher was? And if he is, did yuh know it when yuh come up there in the canyon after him?"

"Of course," answered Clawsuss evenly. "I'd knowed it fer a good many y'ars. And Mark knowed it then, too. That was why we come after him, we wanted tuh get him away afore he turned loose and killed somebody else."

Single-Shot Andy glanced at the rest of The Gang. None of those men was slow witted. In that instant as they stood there in Clawsuss' room, gazing at each other, their minds went back over the years and the little mysteries and events that had puzzled them. They remembered how Butcher Krantz had said that some day he would come to Canyon Center. They remembered, too, how often they had wondered why Clawsuss had come there and built his isolated cabin, and had remained in it, a grim recluse, like a man doggedly and patiently waiting for something—*or somebody.* They knew now for whom he had been waiting; they knew now why the forbidding prison-like character of that staunch cabin. But what the Butcher ever had been to Clawsuss, what the score to settle, they knew they never would know. The lips of the giant were sealed upon that subject and no man in The Gang was fool enough to ask a question to sate his curiosity.

"But why did he kill Crook?" demanded Horse-Pistol Mike. "What had Crook ever done to him?"

"It was Crook who hit him over the head down in Californy," answered Clawsuss quietly. "Crook tried tuh kill him, and always thought he had killed him."

"So *that's* why Crook wasn't afraid of the Butcher!" ejaculated Single-Shot. "He thought he'd killed him."

"Too damn bad he didn't make a better job of it," said Clawsuss. "Because now Mark's had tuh go out after him, and the Butcher's like tuh lead him a long and tough chase afore he ever gets back."

Jo-Anne repressed a little cry, and Andy and The Gang all looked uncomfortably sympathetic, suddenly aware that Jo-Anne had a strong personal interest in Mark Alvord. And Clawsuss sighed and turned away his head. But not to one of them did it occur to think that only a few miles away, close on the heels of Satan, Mark Alvord might be turned that way even now. He was. Following the trail of the Butcher he was riding straight toward Buckshot Canyon, the Great Dane but a few yards in the lead.

CHAPTER XXIX
HELL'S GATE

THE chase was fast drawing to a close, but Mark did not yet know it. He did not even suspect it, till the huge dog, directly ahead of him, suddenly stopped short and growled, his hackles rising, his nose trained on the ground.

"By God, he's gittin' close!" ejaculated Mark.

Satan had, after much weaving and spasmodic advance, come into the lower reaches of Buckshot Canyon itself, over a mile below Hell's Gate. And now the tired dog forgot his weariness, stimulated by the strength of the olfactory clew he had just discovered. His lean body quivered from muscle to haunch. Again he growled deep in his throat, mouthing the sound as if he were worrying a bone. Then, with a sharp whine, he leaped ahead and shot straight down Buckshot Canyon.

With an excited curse Mark spurred the roan horse after the dog.

This time the trail was fresh, the scent new, and the dog loped ahead as animatedly as if he had just begun the chase. He continued straight down

Buckshot Canyon for perhaps a half mile, then he swerved and took a zigzag course up the slope to the ridge at the right. Mark followed on. Across the ridge, into the adjoining gulch and across to another ridge they drove. There again the dog swerved and took his way down a long canyon which ran parallel with Buckshot. For nearly a mile the nameless canyon continued in the same direction, then it made a sharp bend to the north and ran directly away from the location of Buckshot Canyon.

It continued at this angle for a good mile, and the dog followed its course with an ease that proved how clear the scent remained. They had reached a spot some five miles from Hell's Gate when they came upon one of those strange examples of nature's fondness for duplication. Opening off this main canyon were three good-sized side canyons, in close succession, like great gashes dug there by some capricious god for the amusement of the thing.

Less than two hundred yards from the mouth, each of those raying side canyons divided into a fan of four deep draws. Each side canyon with its four heavily wooded draws was so identically like the other two, so lacking in all character, that a man would experience a great deal of difficulty in distinguishing one from the other.

Without hesitation Satan swerved and darted down the third of the side canyons. Mark followed him frantically, recklessly urging Smoke over neck-breaking bowlders, between trees, through down-timber and up steep hillsides, and sometimes the dog was out of sight, but always ahead there rose Satan's deep-throated bay.

This was a territory even more isolated and obscure than Buckshot Canyon. The Butcher had chosen his hiding place well. Without some such ally as Satan no man could possibly follow him into this place, into a terrain as lacking in all identifying landmarks and as monotonous in formation as a honeycomb. And it occurred to Mark even as he rode that Butcher Krantz nor any one else could have retreated to such a hiding place unless he had been there before and knew his way about. This was the place to which the Butcher had retreated after killing Crook. He had not been headed for Hell's Gate at all. And now curiosity rose to spur Mark's fury and passion for vengeance.

What could the Butcher be doing reserving a refuge in this forlorn, forsaken spot in the hills? Mark's gaze narrowed on the excited dog.

Down the second of the four fanning draws Satan led the way. At every yard's advance, more and more Mark realized that any man who retreated to a refuge from pursuers here must know the territory well, must have landmarks so positive that no confusion would be possible. And he felt that for some reason there was significance in the fact, but as yet he could not see why or how.

His puzzlement and impatience were tinged with some relief, relief that the Butcher after all had not been bound for Hell's Gate. Though further thought had uncovered to him the fallacy of Crook's reasoning regarding the probable return of the murderer to Clawsuss' dwelling place. Of course the man would not return there to seek some explanation for the flask of nuggets Clawsuss had failed to produce, or for any unexplained thing concerning Clawsuss himself, because when his memory returned regarding Crook it would return in full, and he himself would know more than any one else could tell him. He would certainly plan to return to the cabin in Buckshot Canyon to dispatch the man who knew him for what he was, regardless of the fact that that man was his brother.

Yet, stay, now—*would* he? Mark leaned to Smoke's wicked jolting and reckless speed, and his brain was in a turmoil. In a very few moments now, if Satan was running true to form, Mark would come face to face with the Butcher, for the final accounting of that black renegade's career. What kind of being was he going to confront? Just how much of the dark alleyways of his life would the Butcher remember? Would he know why he, Mark Alvord, was on his trail? It really mattered very little, Mark told himself savagely. At least the slaughterer would remember the thing he had done to Crook, and that was passport to the gates of hell enough for any man.

That the slayer he was hunting down in the name of justice was brother to Clawsuss had become a factor relegated far to the back of Mark's mind. He rode and acted in the furtherance of justice alone, and he viewed the object of his mission as dispassionately as if the criminal had been a mad dog. Norman Symone deserved no consideration, merited no tear of regret. He was an asset to nothing and a profit to none. He was a menace to society, a menace which must be removed. Mark Alvord was the instrument which presently should remove him, and it was not in Mark's nature to flinch. There was in him no reluctance to the deed. The time for that had passed. The Butcher had passed beyond the pale, had become Butcher Krantz alone, had forfeited all other individuality.

He was no man's brother—and no man's friend.

Mark's grim and judicial thoughts were interrupted by a sudden burst of furious barking from around a sharp bend of the draw dead ahead. It was a roar that always rolled from Satan's throat when he had succeeded in cornering his quarry. Mark jerked out a grim curse and frantically urged his tired horse to one last spurt of speed. Smoke responded with a straining effort, and Mark rose in his stirrups and leaned forward. He heard a man's harsh startled outcry, a shot, and for a moment he felt a wince of panic. Satan! The Butcher had shot

Satan. But Satan's roar continued in unabated fury. Apparently the shot had missed him.

Mark dashed around the bend—and dragged Smoke to a staggering halt.

It was a strange scene that met his eye. To his left rose the slope of the draw, very close. The draw was less heavily timbered here than it was toward the mouth where it debouched toward the canyon. On that left slope was an area that caught Mark's eye and held it, for an extremely unusual sight lay before him.

Roughly in the center of the area, slightly over twenty feet up the moderately steep ascent of the slope, was a good-sized irregular ledge. From the ledge the wall rose in a very steep slant for sixty feet or more. Downward from the ledge a mass of earth and rock lay heaped in a precipitous mass, and the whole area had a peculiar look of unnaturalness about it. Something in the formation was not now as nature had intended it to be, nor as she herself had created it. That thought prodded Mark's consciousness, as his sweeping glance flashed over the scene. Some inner corner of his mind caught and registered details as automatically and faithfully as a camera lens records light and shade on a negative.

And abruptly Mark saw what it was that was not natural.

All around the area the timber was old and tall, great first growth thick-boled trees reared through ancient brush clumps, as they had reared no doubt for centuries. All *around* the area they were so, yes. But within the area itself the trees were few, and those few were slim boled, had as yet not reached any very considerable height, so that they were dwarfed by the bigger trees surrounding them. None was more than seventeen or eighteen years old. There was plenty of evidence that bigger trees had been there. Stumps and felled logs in several places told the story of the vanishing of the older timber from the spot. Something like nineteen or twenty years ago some one had cleared this plot of land.

The ledge itself was the thing that was not natural. That is, it was not natural in that place. These were not slopes commonly broken by ledges. The formation was not characteristic of the terrain. Of course, a ledge might occur anywhere—but not a ledge such as this. The very position in which the rock and earth lay heaped gave the clew to any man who was familiar with earth and rocks and the ways of the elements. This ledge had been made neither by the original cast of creation nor by the action of erosion. It had been made by dynamite.

The man who had done the blasting had used plenty of the explosive to accomplish his purpose, he had used enough to be certain of the amount of dirt and rock he was tearing down. But why should any one go to the trouble of clearing a patch of land here on a draw slope where the labor must be slow and arduous, then deliberately dynamite a large part of the slope down into the cleared spot?

Mechanically Mark's brain clicked into place the numerous details and facts that lay bare to his observing eye, drew the obvious conclusions and asked the involuntary question of himself, instinctively and instantly, in that first swift sweeping glance he sent up and down, over and across the slope.

But he did not consciously stop to reason it all out, did not waste any precious fraction of time in thinking of anything at all that went beyond what his eyes saw and what his ears heard. His eyes made that one flashing survey of the entire scene, then fixed intent and sharply scrutinizing, on the man standing on the ledge with a drawn gun in his hand, shouting fiercely at the great dog menacing him.

Mark had seen Norman Symone close at hand and in numberless attitudes, had lived in the same house with him for days and had watched him with curious and interested eyes. He had become thoroughly familiar with the man's face, with all its lines and planes and expressions. He had studied Symone's countenance to that end. But he scarcely would have known the bestial features of the man on the ledge for those of the same person with whom he had been in such close contact for several days.

It was not the same person. This was, in reality,

a man Mark Alvord had never seen before, but a man with whom Clawsuss must have been altogether too familiar for comfort. This was Butcher Krantz, than whom no greater scoundrel had ever lived, of whom nothing too base could be said, the man who had been terror and scourge to the frontier for so long. He looked it. His features were convulsed with fury, his skin was livid, his lips were writhed back from his teeth in a snarl, his eyes blazed with that same light which burns in the orbs of the predatory beast on the kill.

Both his drawn gun and his abusing curses were directed to the Great Dane. Less than ten feet below him, Satan crouched behind a bowlder. The dog's first leap up the slope had precipitated him there, and there he lay now, flat on his belly, his hackles stiff, his jaws slavering, his maddened roar unabated. Satan had been taught to dodge to cover when guns crashed and bullets whined. Only once in his life had the dog taken a bullet, and that had been when he had tried to leap upon Mark and Mark had downed him. He had known even as he leaped that he was making a mistake, that this man was his master. He had known it still better when Mark's gun laid him low. Never again had he tried to leap upon Mark. He had learned a healthy fear of Mark's guns. In addition to which Mark had taught him to protect himself from other men's guns.

The Butcher was his quarry. In another leap or

two he could have thrown himself upon the man. But he knew that motion of the hand too well, the motion Mark had patiently taught him to know, and even as the Butcher's hand moved, the huge dog flattened himself behind the bowlder and the bullet whined harmlessly over his head.

Evidently the Butcher had been hard at work on the ledge when the dog burst into sight. Evidences of his activities were numerous. A hastily discarded pick lay tilted against a heap of earth and small rocks beside him. The heap was fresh and raw, showing how recently it had been piled there. Beyond him, into the slope close down to the ledge, a hole yawned, a good-sized hole, easily six by eight feet. He had been very busy indeed; so busy, so utterly absorbed, that his intentness and the clatter of his own labors, the ring of his pick upon rock and the rattle of disturbed rubble had dulled his ears to other sounds. He had not become aware of the dog's approach till Satan had burst into that full-throated roar of fury, that bay of triumph at seeing his quarry within easy reach.

Satan had even reached the foot of the slope and made that one long leap, before the Butcher came out of his startled trance enough to realize that it was he whom the beast was trailing.

It was then he had dashed aside his pick, whipped out his gun and fired. It was then Satan had flattened to safety behind the bowlder. It was then Mark had flashed into sight and drawn Smoke to that staggering halt.

The Butcher's gaze jerked to Mark, and he scowled, and a look of surprise and resentment crossed his bestial features. At first he had not expected to see any one following the dog. For an instant he had thought that the excited brute must be running down a deer; twice he had seen him and heard him doing that very thing, when he had been staying at Hell's Gate, and the dog's actions had been much the same then as now. But when Satan swerved and started up the slope, it was borne in upon the man abruptly that it was no deer the dog trailed, that it was himself, and that some man must have set the Dane to the chase.

And the Butcher had glared at the bend of the draw in triumphant anticipation, lusting to satisfy at last that envious hatred he had always felt for George.

It nonplussed him for a moment that it was not George who appeared there, but Mark. But he was berserk enough so that he anticipated eagerly the very act of killing something, and he wet his lips avidly at the thought. Mark Alvord, eh? Brother to that deformed ape who had tried to kill him in California, and had come hellishly near doing it, and had paid the price paid by all fools who attempted assault on the Butcher. The murderer glared down at Mark, gloating, infinitely pleased at the opportunity for putting out of the way the brother of Crook, before he went on to Hell's Gate to settle George's case once and for all. He couldn't have asked for a better setup. Couldn't have hoped for things to play more into his hands. He had the whole affair in his own control and no danger of a slip.

There *couldn't* be any slip. Alvord sat there on his weary horse, motionless, a perfect target, and Norman Symone, alias Butcher Krantz, had him covered.

The Butcher shouted something, but Mark could not hear him above the dog's enraged roar. "Shut up, Satan!" commanded Mark, and the dog's barking subsided to a whine that was literally a moan of fury. Mark's gaze did not waver from the Butcher's face. "Did you say something?" he asked curtly, cool and unflustered, playing for time, maneuvering for that bare instant of advantage that would give him a chance with the man who already had him covered with the drawn gun.

"I said, 'So it's only you,' " the Butcher informed him contemptuously. "I was expecting to see George—or Clawsuss, as you call him. Funny these men you lay out don't always stay dead, isn't it? I was so damn certain I'd killed him as dead as Greggory—only I didn't know he was George then. And that bastard brother of yours was so sure he'd killed me in California. He nearly did it, too, damn him. And just looking at his face brought me out of that half dead state he'd knocked me into.

Kind of inconvenient when these dead men come to life, isn't it?"

"Sometimes."

Mark sat there on Smoke, staring up into the Butcher's face as coolly as if he did not realize, quite, that within a very few seconds that gun was going to belch and his flesh was going to feel the bite of lead. He wasn't wasting any time worrying about it. He was getting set in the saddle, freeing the muscles in his arm to the move, alert to the instant when his hands should flash to the guns he had oiled into perfect working order. He knew he could not escape or elude the bullet which the Butcher would presently loose upon him. Very likely he would forfeit his life to the grim demand of circumstance. The one thought he had was to be so prepared for the move that he would act as an automaton, that his brain would still command, that his hands would still act, that the Butcher should not escape. He was steeling himself for the jar of the bullet, so that sheer bulletshock should not deter him and spoil his aim. His eyes bored into the Butcher's face. He said brusquely:

"Yes. Sometimes. Damned inconvenient. What are you going to do about it?"

The Butcher laughed, the same laugh George Symone had heard when the slayer walked out of the cabin thinking he was leaving both George and Cass Greggory equally dead. The Butcher was thinking of that time, now, as he stood on the ledge and stared, gloating, down at Mark. "So he remembered that I said I'd meet him at Hell's Gate, did he? Well, I always keep my word. I said I'd come to Canyon Center someday. I came."

"You should have said you'd come *back* to Canyon Center," Mark corrected, and his words dripped acid. They were fulgurous with meaning. He was still playing for time.

The Butcher started slightly. "*Back* to Canyon Center?" he repeated. "How the hell did you know I'd ever been here before?"

Mark laughed shortly. "No man could come to this spot, for refuge or for any other thing, who hadn't been here before, many times, and who hadn't marked his way minutely." Mark was feeling his way, choosing his words, jockeying for that hair's-breadth chance. He had no hope that the Butcher would be taken off guard. The Butcher wasn't that kind of man. He was so sure of himself that he hadn't even commanded Mark to put up his hands. It wasn't necessary. With his uncanny skill and speed, he was safe. He was no bungler. He was just sure enough of himself that he might be made a hair's breadth too sure. He *was that* kind of man. For that Mark played, a desperate game. He went on evenly:

"You don't really think you'll get away with this, do you? You got Crook, and you'll likely get me. You may even get Clawsuss. But you'll never get Satan. Satan will trail you to hell and back, and the men of Canyon Center will all see behind your false face, will know you for who you are. They aren't fools enough to believe Satan could be wrong."

"Oh, yeah?" the Butcher laughed rather loudly. "Men in a little town like this can be made to believe anything. They even believed me a good many years ago when I told them I'd lost my mine and couldn't find it again. I wasn't idiot enough to let the whole damn country in on a strike like that. So I ducked out, intending to come back and clean the mine later when nobody knew anything about it. I never figured on visiting Canyon Center— officially, let us say. And I'd have been back here long ago if it hadn't been for that crook-backed brother of yours. But that's none of your damn business, and following me up here is less of it. I've too much to do, I have to collect and get out of here. I can't waste time with men of your kidney. I told that poor simpleton I'd meet him at Hell's Gate, and I can't break my word. He'd probably be lonesome down there without you. You can go ahead to keep the pitch hot."

Mark's gaze was fixed unwinking on the man's whole figure, mostly on his eyes and on the finger curled around the trigger of the pointing gun. He saw that indefinable set of muscle on the bestial countenance, that indescribable preface to action that warned him. The Butcher was very sure of himself as his finger cinched on the trigger. The gun barked. The lead went true. The Butcher was so sure that he couldn't miss. He didn't.

Yet the Butcher was twenty feet above his target, and in making sure that he should not shoot too low, he shot too high. The Butcher hadn't been doing much shooting for several years.

Mark felt the thud of the lead, like a light blow, high to the shoulder on the left side. Mark didn't know much about anatomy, but he did know enough to realize that the shot was too high to have touched the heart. He felt an infinitesimal flash of panic in which he wondered if the ball had pierced a lung.

And in the same instant, as his brain reacted to the alarm of an injured lung, his hands moved with the skill and celerity of muscles trained by long practice. The Butcher had not believed that any man on earth could match skill with him. He had an instant of stark shock and terror in which he saw both of Mark's hands training the black muzzles of guns upon him. He couldn't understand it. Why didn't Mark fall from his horse? He had been so certain he hit him.

He even had an instant of incredulity; it wasn't possible that any man was as fast as he. But he was to learn. Before that tearing slug of lead had passed through Mark's body and fallen spent to the rocks behind him somewhere, both Mark's guns firing alternately and repeatedly, had blasted their fury and retribution upon the murderer on the ledge.

It seemed to the Butcher that some one struck him upon the chest, a jarring hard blow. He felt suddenly as foolishly weak as if his bones had turned to water. His legs twisted under him, and he had no ability to command them. He swayed and whirled half around, like a dummy figure jerked about by an unseen hand. He made a colossal effort to right himself, to retain his balance, but he had been shaken too far from his equilibrium to recover his footing. He staggered, strove frenziedly for a moment to regain a hold on the ledge, then pitched over the edge, clawing at the rock with one hand, with the other striving to raise his gun to firing position as he came rattling down.

With the wild roar of a demon released, Satan leaped.

Which was one time when not even the voice of Mark Alvord could turn the Great Dane from his purpose.

Mark turned his head, averting his gaze, and his eyes lifted to the white morning sky into which the sun was wheeling. He hadn't much idea about the hereafter. He wasn't too sure what he knew about God, or whether or not people had souls. He did believe that nothing died utterly, particularly people, especially if they were good people: somewhere, somehow, something imperishable lived on. Whatever it was, it stood for the person gone before—like Crook. Maybe Crook could see him, from that somewhere. Maybe he could hear.

He thought of that mutilated body that had been all there was remaining of Crook. He shuddered, as he spoke aloud. "He's going to be good and dead this time, Crook. He's on his way to Hell's Gate, all right, but not to meet Clawsuss, nor you. There's plenty of others waiting there for him. Satan! Come here! You hear me, damn you! Come here. Quiet, now. Shut up. It's done. Yeah, Crook—good and dead."

He studiously avoided looking at the remains of the Butcher, though in spite of himself he could see the still cadaver lying there where Satan had left it, the senseless body with its throat torn wide open, with the last of the blood in the veins pumping from the severed jugular into the rocky soil. There was a dead man who would never rise and walk again.

Mark swung down from Smoke's back, slowly re-holstering his guns, and with one hand he wiped his face—a queer, agonized gesture, as if he had sweat blood and it was stinging his eyes. He was conscious of the fact that blood from his own wound was wetting his shirt, not much, but enough to tell him that it was there, and to remind him that he must get to Hell's Gate with speed and caution. He felt a little dizzy and faint, and again he wondered if the ball had touched a lung.

He glanced up at the ledge, at the yawning hole the Butcher had dug there. Not much need to look into that hole: he felt certain he knew what was within. He had known since the moment in which he had seen Symone standing there with his pick. Probably it had been the confusing formation of the canyon and draws that had given the Butcher the idea in the first place, the idea of going into town and telling everybody that he couldn't find his rich mine again. And when some of them had been generous enough to volunteer to aid him, he had taken them to hunt for it in the opposite direction from that in which it lay.

Just to keep a gold rush away from his claim? Solely to hoard that source of wealth to himself in secret?

"Mmmm—maybe," Mark muttered, staring up at the ledge. "But it don't hold water. It ain't the natural thing for a man to do. There was more to it than that—though I don't suppose any one will ever know what it was. It's likely useless, all right, but I'm going to have one look into that hole before I leave here. I may never get back. Maybe I'm going on a long journey, too. But—I'll go alone. I ain't going any way he went. Satan, lie down there and stay till I come back."

He turned from the dog and walked along the heap of earth and rock till he came to fairly easy ascent, and made his way up the slope, carefully and rather laboriously, to the hole Symone had dug. And when he had reached it he stood still, staring into it. Symone had opened up what seemed to be a small natural cavern, reaching back into the slope, the mouth of which he had hidden by a blast so long ago. Inside the hole another sloping heap of rock led downward to the floor of the open space, making an easy descent. Mark stepped into the opening, and walked carefully down to the floor, and he saw now that it had been stoutly lined with timbering. It was not a cavern.

It was a low tunnel cutting into the hill. A miner's tunnel, and it had not been made by any green young tyro new to the ways of a mining land. It had been made by an experienced man who knew what he was doing.

Mark frowned and looked about him. The hole did not let in a great deal of light, and Mark saw nothing of any significance within the visible space. He drew from his pocket a piece of the paper he had had wrapped about some of the cooked food, twisted it into a taper and lighted it. Holding it high, he advanced a way into the tunnel, and looked about again—and again he stopped short.

The rest of the story lay there before him, in mute objects that still spoke eloquently. A miner's pick was dug into the rock, where it had been sent in a powerful blow by a man hard at work. The man himself lay by it, on his face—all that was left of him, a moldering skeleton. A small hand ax was buried deep in the back of the skull. The man had been killed as he bent over his labor. He had been killed so instantly that he had never known what struck him.

The skeleton lay undisturbed, as it had been through all the years. A few tatters of rotted cloth still remained of the clothes. The boot, save for a little mildew and a warped sole, looked as if it might have been left there yesterday. The boot. Yes. There was only one boot. The other leg had been cut off a little way above the knee. By that short piece of femur bone lay an old hand-whittled artificial limb. It had been fastened into place with a piece of harness breeching.

The linen thread had rotted away, but the padded harness breeching remained warped to the mold it had taken about the man's thigh.

Mark stood still and stared down at the mute accuser, the evidence of one of the earliest crimes of Butcher Krantz. "So he was the first one, eh?" Mark said aloud. "Poor old Pegleg Miller; made his strike after all, only to lose it to a fellow that was born to kill. No wonder that damned fiend wanted to get away from here and lie low. Good reason he didn't dare let anybody come out to his rich mine. No wonder he blasted rock down over the mouth of the tunnel and left it till a few years passed and he dared to come back. Them old timers would have known in a minute that no green kid ever drove this drift." And he shook his head, aghast at the abysmal baseness of the man he had executed so that justice might not be altogether cheated.

He shook his head, and realized that he still felt

dizzy, and that the air in the old tunnel was foul, and that he should be going. He retraced his steps back to the mouth of the bore, up the heap of earth and rocks, through the hole and down from the ledge, to where Satan waited him patiently.

He found it a little difficult to get into the saddle, but being what he was he accomplished it. Then he turned Smoke's head and set his face blindly toward Hell's Gate.

CHAPTER XXX
EL DORADO

IT was an hour later that Jo-Anne, watching feverishly from one of the living room windows, saw him coming up Buckshot Canyon. She cried out, and whirled away from the window, and went running toward the door.

Clawsuss, who was feeling much more like himself than he had been, having eaten a hearty breakfast and drunk plenty of strong coffee at her orders, had ensconced himself in a chair before the fireplace, his favorite easy chair, because he said he had to sit up or go crazy of restlessness. As Jo-Anne cried out and started toward the door, he roused and called after her.

"What's up, ma'am? Is he comin'?"

He meant Mark. They were, all of them, interested in the coming of no one else. The others were still in the kitchen eating breakfast, but they had heard Jo-Anne's cry, the patter of her running feet, and Clawsuss' question. They heard her answer.

"Yes!" She called back over her shoulder, as she reached the door and wrenched it open. She paused for just an instant, to add: "And he's either ready to drop of weariness, or he's hurt. I think he's hurt. I don't like the way he rides. Andy! Pete! Somebody come quickly!"

She dashed across the porch, leaped to the ground, ignoring the convenience of the steps, and went running to meet Mark with all the speed of which she was capable.

Cobalt and Single-Shot Andy came rushing from the kitchen door in response to her call, the others of The Gang close behind. Blue, bringing up the rear, paused by Clawsuss, and at a word from Yellowjacket the others held back lest they be in the way, while Cobalt and Andy dashed out the door in pursuit of Jo-Anne. As they crossed the porch they saw that she was already halfway there to meet the advancing horseman.

Smoke was coming at a slow walk, Satan, tongue lolling, plodding patiently at his side. Mark was striving to sit erect and nonchalant in the saddle, not making too good a job of it. He pulled the roan horse to a halt, a little smile growing on his face, as Jo-Anne rushed up to him.

But she did not see the smile. She saw the splotches of blood on his light tan shirt. She saw the haggard circles around his lead-gray eyes. She saw the lines of pain and weariness in his drawn face. She caught Smoke's bridle and stared up at him.

"Don't try to get down! Andy and Pete will lift you down. Oh—Mark! Have you come back again only to go away from me?"

He knew what she meant. The smile grew tender. He shook his head. "I don't think so, Jo, girl. I'm pretty tough."

She saw the smile then, and she saw the changing expression on his face, and the quick tears started to her eyes. "How did you manage to get away? Who—who did it?"

"The Butcher. He was the one who didn't get away."

But there Cobalt and Single-Shot reached him, and he gave a little sigh of relief and weariness as they reached up their arms and eased him to the ground. They insisted that they were going to carry him into the house. He didn't object. He was too greatly interested in the phenomenon of finding himself the center of interest. As the two men entered the living room with him, Clawsuss sat erect in his chair, the very picture of anxiety and concern. Blue stepped forward, scrutinizing the injured man with anxious eyes.

Yellowjacket Bevans and Shy Bolcom rushed to get the two easiest chairs together, close to Clawsuss, to serve as a makeshift bed. Horse-Pistol Mike rushed into Clawsuss' bedroom to get an armful of quilts to pad the chairs for Mark's greater comfort. Highway Bill dashed into Blue's room to get another pillow; the two Mike had brought from Clawsuss' room weren't enough. Ike Pratt raced into the kitchen to replenish the fire and put on fresh coffee. Windy Lucas and Spade Lowry hurried into Clawsuss' storeroom and came out lugging a gallon jug of whisky. One would have thought from the actions of The Gang that they were competing with each other to see which could do the most for Mark Alvord.

But Mark understood. They had misjudged, had adopted a belligerent attitude toward him and Clawsuss. They had been ready to hang him. This was their apology. It was all the apology they would ever make. But it was enough. Mark accepted their ministrations and attentions with a sober but hearty gratitude that was tacit acceptance of their apology. But all his eyes were for Jo-Anne.

She had, at Blue's quick order, produced a pair of scissors, and a pan of hot water, and was busily but carefully cutting away the bloodied shirt from about the shoulder so that Blue might examine the wound.

"I've done a little rough first aid work, in my time, since I've been out here. Had to," Blue told Mark, eyeing the wound closely as Jo-Anne cut away the last of the cloth front and back. He bent down, feeling deftly on each side of the shoulder, as Jo-Anne washed away the blood and left the skin clean, the bullet hole fully exposed. Blue finally straightened himself with a little whistle of surprise and relief. "Man, but you're a lucky cuss. The ball cut on a slight slant, the fellow must have been above you when he shot. But the lead cut clean, between the scapula and the clavicle, and, as you might say, never touched you."

"Use plain English, will yuh?" Clawsuss put in.

Blue grinned at Mark. "I mean the bullet went through that little round hole between the collar bone and the shoulder blade. Couldn't have picked a neater spot to cut a clean hole and do less damage. There's nothing the matter with you. Look at that shirt—didn't even lose much blood. The wound was sort of cauterized by the speed of the bullet. You must have been pretty close to him. I know, you feel dizzy and weak—but that's from worry and strain, and loss of sleep, and hunger. Ike will have some coffee and grub in here for you pronto. You go ahead and clean him up, Jo-Anne. Make you both feel better. I'll go out and see if I can do anything to help Ike."

Clawsuss was studying Mark with burning eyes, and as Blue turned away he asked the question that would no longer be denied. "You—yuh caught him?"

And suddenly the room went still, and all the little activities ceased, and every man was listening, waiting for the answer.

"Yeah," said Mark steadily. "Don't ask—too

much. The account's closed. It was him that started the legend about the Lost Cabin Mine, so many years ago, him who come to town tellin' the windy about not bein' able to find it again, and leadin' the whole town in the *opposite* direction to look for it. Good reason he didn't want the town messing around there. Good reason he ducked out of Canyon Center, after blasting some rock down to hide a tunnel into the hillside. The skeleton of Peg-leg Miller is lying in there now, an ax buried in the skull.

"After killing Crook, the Butcher went to his old mine to hide. You can—you can put all worry out of your mind. He'll never butcher anybody again. Somebody can go up there after while, and kind of put him away. I can tell anybody how to get there. You—you keep a stiff upper lip, if you can. You and me—we're in the same boat. I ain't got no brother any more, either."

Cobalt started at the word *brother,* realizing that Mark could not know Clawsuss' desire that the rest of The Gang be kept in ignorance of the Butcher's relationship to him, wondering if the unmistakable meaning of what Mark had just said would miss the other men. He flashed a glance at Clawsuss, and in the same instant he saw the look that went from man to man. They had caught it, but no man would ever know it from them. And Clawsuss saw that too, and let it rest there. He gazed back at Mark levelly.

"Oh, yes yuh have," he contradicted. "Yuh've got me."

Something happened to Mark Alvord's face. He heard the patter of small feet, as Petey, just awakened, came trotting downstairs to see if everything was all right with his honest-to-Gawd man-sized dawg. He saw all The Gang standing about, trying to find something to do next. He saw Blue and Ike Pratt coming in from the kitchen with steaming food and coffee. And Highway Bill insisted that he should have a good stout drink of whisky first before he ate. And Blue grinned and winked at him and said he thought it might be a good idea. Friends. All of them. Friends of his.

Was he the man who could never make friends? All the hunger and loneliness were gone from his face. He smiled at Clawsuss. Brother.

And at last his lingering gaze lifted to Jo-Anne, and stayed there. The yearning and the bewilderment died forever from the lead-gray eyes, and the little cold light that had always been there glowed and grew warm. Love, friendship, home. After many long paths and devious ways, Mark Alvord had come into his Never-never Land.

Center Point Publishing
600 Brooks Road ● PO Box 1
Thorndike ME 04986-0001 USA

(207) 568-3717

US & Canada:
1 800 929-9108
www.centerpointlargeprint.com